MOON

of the

CRUSTED
SNOW

A Novel

WAUBGESHIG RICE

Published by ECW Press
665 Gerrard Street East
Toronto, ON M4M 1Y2
416-694-3348 / ecwpress.com

Editor for the press: Susan Renouf
Cover design: Michel Vrana
Cover artwork: © David Caesar /
www.davidcaesar.com
Author photo: Shilo Adamson

Printing: Marquis   8

Purchase the print edition
and receive the ebook free!
For details, go to ecwpress.com/ebook.

LIBRARY AND ARCHIVES CANADA CATALOGUING
IN PUBLICATION

Rice, Waubgeshig, 1979-, author
Moon of the crusted snow : a novel /
Waubgeshig Rice.
Issued in print and electronic formats.

ISBN 978-1-77041-400-6 (softcover).—ISBN
978-1-77305-244-1 (HTML).—
ISBN 978-1-77305-245-8 (PDF)
I. Title.

PS8635.I246M66 2018   C813'.6   C2018-902543-
3
C2018-902544-1

MIX
Paper from
responsible sources
FSC® C103567

The publication of Moon of the Crusted Snow has been generously supported by the Canada
Council for the Arts which last year invested $153 million to bring the arts to Canadians throughout
the country, and by the Government of Canada. *Nous remercions le Conseil des arts du Canada de
son soutien. L'an dernier, le Conseil a investi 153 millions de dollars pour mettre de l'art dans la vie des
Canadiennes et des Canadiens de tout le pays. Ce livre est financé en partie par le gouvernement du
Canada.* We also acknowledge the Ontario Arts Council (OAC), an agency of the Government of
Ontario, and the contribution of the Government of Ontario through the Ontario Book Publishing
Tax Credit and the Ontario Media Development Corporation.

Ontario
Ontario Media Development
Corporation

ONTARIO ARTS COUNCIL
CONSEIL DES ARTS DE L'ONTARIO
an Ontario government agency
un organisme du gouvernement de l'Ontario

Canada Council
for the Arts

Conseil des Arts
du Canada

Canada

Printed and bound in Canada

To my son, Jiikwis,
who shines a bright and beautiful light on our future.

PART ONE

DAGWAAGIN
AUTUMN

ONE

A crack echoed through the boreal landscape, a momentary chaos in the still afternoon air. In the near distance, a large bull moose fell to its side. Evan Whitesky stood and looped his rifle around his right shoulder, adjusted his neon orange hat, and began a slow walk over to his kill. The smell of gunpowder briefly dominated the crisp scent of impending winter.

His grey boots pushed through the yellowing grass of the glade. Evan was pleased. He had been out since early morning and had been tracking this particular bull since around noon. The fall hunt was drawing to a close, and he still wanted to put more food away. Food from the South was expensive and never as good, or as satisfying, as the meat he could bring in himself.

By the time Evan reached the moose moments later, it was dead. Massive antlers propped up its head. The eyes were open, vacant, and the bull's long tongue flopped out onto the grass. Evan reached into the right pocket of his cargo pants and pulled out a small leather pouch faded and smooth from years of wear. He brought it up to just below his chest and balanced it in the centre of his palm. He ran his thumb across the small beaded pattern in the middle, feeling where the beads were missing in the simple bear design. *I'll ask Auntie to re-bead this later this fall*, he thought.

Evan looked down at the beautiful design: a black bear in a red circle edged in white. At least half the outer white beads were gone and there was a bald patch near the bear's head and hind legs. Most of the beaded bear itself remained, though. He untied the leather string and pinched some tobacco into his open palm. It came from a plastic pouch of rolling tobacco he bought at the trading post on the way out — he'd forgotten to get the dry, untreated tobacco, or semaa, from his medicine bundle before leaving the house. The shredded, manufactured leaves seemed to gum together. He bounced the tiny heap in his left hand before wrapping his fingers around it. He closed his eyes.

"Gchi-manidoo," he said aloud. "Great spirit, today I say miigwech for the life you have given us." He inhaled deeply and paused. This was still a little new to him. "Miigwech for my family. And for my community. Miigwech for our health. Chi-miigwech for the life you have allowed me to take today, this moozoo, to feed my family." He still felt a little awkward, saying this prayer of thanks mostly in English, with only a few Ojibwe words peppered here and there. But it still made him feel good to believe that he was giving back in some way.

Evan expressed thanks for the good life he was trying to lead. He apologized for not being able to pray fluently in his native language and asked for a bountiful fall hunting season for everyone. He promised to keep trying to live in a good way, despite the pull of negative influences around him. He finished his prayer with a resounding, solitary miigwech before putting the tobacco on the ground in front of the moose. This was his offering of gratitude to the Creator and Mother Earth for allowing him to take this life. As he took from the earth, he gave back. It was the Anishinaabe way, as he understood it.

His head was clear. The adrenaline surge of the kill was brief, as was his remorse for taking a life. Evan had spent nearly his whole life hunting. His father had first taught him to identify and follow moose tracks in the deep bush around their reserve when he was five. Now, nearly twenty years later, he was on his own, tracking his own kill to support his young family. When he was new to the hunt, the sympathy and sadness he felt after pulling the trigger lasted days. Now he was a father himself and necessity overcame reluctance and regret.

This is a big fella, he thought. He looked over the bull once more before turning back to where he'd parked his four-wheeler deeper in the bush that morning. He would have to butcher the animal here; it was too big for him to heft onto his ATV's trailer by himself. On some hunts, he would leave his kill on the land overnight and return the next day with help. But he didn't have any tarps or blankets with him to cover up the moose and mask its scent from other predators. And the chill in the air told him that he should move quickly.

A deep orange glow coated the northern landscape as the sun began to set, highlighting the deep evergreen of the pine and spruce trees that towered beyond the ridge. As he walked, the sky above became darker blue, and the air was markedly cooler. Overhead, a small formation of geese broke the silence, complaining about their migration south for the season. *I thought they were all gone*. Had he expected this delayed flock, he would have had his shotgun with him to add to the day's bounty. But he already had a good stock of plucked and halved geese in a freezer at home; it didn't matter that much.

He stepped up to the four-wheeler and straddled it, then turned the key in the ignition. The harsh rumbling of the machine racketed across the field, chasing the soothing off-beat cries of the geese. He hadn't expected to find a moose this close to where he'd first stopped just after dawn. He'd covered vast amounts of open terrain and thick bush throughout the day and he was about to pack it in. But he found a decent spot overlooking the small meadow on the walk back to his vehicle and decided to stop and wait. It had paid off.

The four-wheeler flattened the tall grass as Evan made his way back to the moose. He made a quick inventory of the meat they'd have for the winter: three moose, ten geese, more than thirty fish (trout, pickerel, pike), and four rabbits, for now — more rabbits would be snared through the winter. It was more than enough for his own family of four, but he planned to give a lot of the meat away. It was the community way. He would share with his parents, his siblings and their families, and his in-laws, and would save some for others who might run out before winter's end and not be able to afford the expensive ground beef and chicken thighs that were trucked or flown in from the South.

The thought of eating only packaged meat if all that game ran out made Evan shudder. "Bad moose meat is always better than a good pork chop," his father always said. Evan ate southern meats when he had to, but he felt detached from that food. He'd learned to hunt when he was a boy out of tradition, but also necessity. It was harder than buying store-bought meat but it was more economical and rewarding. Most importantly, hunting, fishing, and living on the land was Anishinaabe custom, and Evan was trying to live in harmony with the traditional ways.

The four-wheeler rolled up to the dead moose. Evan turned it off and reached for the green canvas bag strapped to the rack on the back. He pulled out four large game bags for the smaller cuts of meat and the innards, then tossed the bags on the ground next to the animal and brought out his foldable razor knife. It would be dark soon so he had to cut quickly.

The bull's spoor was strong in his nose as he moved in to bring a hind leg to rest against his torso. He began to cut swiftly and methodically on the inside of the hip, and the skin opened easily, exposing the white tendons and purple muscle beneath. Cutting through further, he pressed against the leg with his opposite shoulder, dislocating the hip joint.

Once he had severed the hindquarter, Evan lugged it over to the trailer. He felt the burn in his arms and shoulders as he heaved the meat over the edge and onto the plywood base. He did this for each limb, arranging them neatly on the wide trailer bed, then he cut the meat from the back and neck, gutted what was left, and filled his game bags.

He would have liked to have kept the hide intact. If his dad and a couple of his cousins or buddies were with him, they could have loaded the whole moose onto a truck and done all the skinning and cleaning at home. There they could clean and eventually tan the hide to use for drums, moccasins, gloves, and clothing.

By the time Evan was finished, the sun had crept below the horizon and it was nearly dark. It wasn't a long trip home and he knew this bush intimately, but he didn't want Nicole to worry, so he steered his vehicle back to the trail that led to his community.

Evan rolled up to the simple rectangular box of his home. The lights were on in the living room but the rest of the house was dark. *The kids must be in bed*, he thought. He pulled up his jacket sleeve to check his watch. It was well past Maiingan's and Nangohns's bedtime. He would see them in the morning.

He backed up to the shed that contained a freezer, a refrigerator, a large wooden table, hanging hooks, and everything else he'd need to finish preparing the moose. It would get cold overnight but not so much that the meat would freeze. He loaded everything inside, shut the heavy door and locked it, and headed into the house.

Evan walked through the front door to an unusual silence. The flat-screen television on the living room wall was off. By now Nicole would usually be watching a sitcom or a crime show. "Aaniin?" Evan announced himself, accentuating the uptick at the end of the word as if to question what was going on.

"Oh, hey," his partner said from around the corner. "You're back."

"It's so quiet in here," Evan replied, taking off his heavy outer layer.

"Yeah, the satellite went out earlier," Nicole said as she stepped into the living room. "I dunno what's going on. Wind musta blew it offline or something."

"That's weird. I thought you'd be laid out on the couch this time of night, as usual," he teased, with a playful smirk.

"As if. So how was it out there?"

"Got another moose."

"Right on!"

"Yeah, it took all day. Didn't see nothing out there all morning. I was gonna give up, then I seen him on my way back to the four-wheeler. Had to quarter him out there. Took longer than I thought."

"We can give some of that to your parents, eh?"

"Yeah, that's what I was thinking."

He untied his boots and stepped out of them before moving

into the living room in his sock feet. "Phone died. Woulda called you to say when I'd be home."

"I figured as much," she said.

Evan reached for the charger cable that lay on the side table by the couch and plugged in his phone. He pulled off his black hoodie and threw it over one of the wooden chairs of the modest table set. In the still indoor air, he noticed his hunger.

"Hey, where's my sugar?" Nicole teased, beckoning for a kiss.

"Oh!" He stepped closer to her, his lips in an exaggerated pucker. He placed his hands softly on her hips and gave her a simple kiss.

"You hungry?" she asked.

"Yeah, I just noticed," he replied. He had finished his last sandwich just before spotting the moose. "That chi-moozoo distracted me, I guess."

"Well, I put a plate in the fridge for you. You just gotta throw it in the microwave. You're lucky the kids saved you some."

She nudged him toward the fridge, and he took out the plate, peeling back the tinfoil covering to reveal a sparsely seasoned chicken leg, mashed potatoes, and frozen peas. His stomach growled as he waited for the meal to heat up.

Evan Whitesky and Nicole McCloud had been in each other's lives since childhood. He could trace the path of his own life by his signpost memories of her, and she could do the same. He remembered the first time he saw her, swimming at the lake the summer before kindergarten began. She wore a light blue bathing suit and her wet hair was tied into a long ponytail. Her older sister Danielle was watching her. Nicole was smiling and laughing.

They crossed paths again on their first day of kindergarten. She still teased him about the awkward outfit he wore that day: baggy overalls and a red T-shirt with fading yellow cartoon characters on the front and a bowl hair cut that made his head look big. He was shy and didn't talk much most of the morning, and shortly before the school day broke at noon, he cried for his mother. He went home with wet cheeks and a runny nose.

Being somewhat unacquainted at such a young age was unusual in a community as small as theirs. Their parents knew one another but weren't close friends or relatives — his mom and her dad both came from different reserves in the South. Basically, they weren't cousins, and that perhaps destined them to bond as curious friends in elementary school and become a couple by high school. Innocent attraction became intense passion and, despite a year apart when Nicole went to college in the South, it eventually evolved into the loving partnership that bore two beautiful young children. The eldest, Maiingan, was five and had school in the morning. Three-year-old Nangohns was still at home with Nicole.

The kids were what pushed Evan through the bush on the hunt. Feeding them always motivated him to see the task through. He still hadn't used up all his allotted hunting days from his maintenance job at the community's public works department, so he decided he'd use the morning to finish dressing the moose. The microwave beeps interrupted his thoughts and he pulled open the door to grab his plate, sitting down across from Nicole, who'd come to the table to join him.

"Well, if the TV's out, looks like you're gonna have to entertain me," he said.

"We might actually have to have a conversation!" she retorted. Her black hair that he loved unbound was pulled back into a tight, practical ponytail and her brown eyes squinted with her laughter. He chuckled and began to eat, careful not to get any mashed potatoes in his patchy black goatee.

"I don't even remember the last time it was quiet like this in here," she said. He nodded. "We should keep the TV and that computer off more often," she continued. "Get the kids outside while we can."

In the coming weeks, the temperature would drop and the snow would come. Soon after, the lake would freeze over and the snow and ice would be with them for six months. Like people in many other northern reserves, they would be isolated by the long, unforgiving season, confined to a small radius around the village that extended only as far as a snowmobile's half tank of gas.

Evan finished eating, and his eyes drooped under the weight of his fatigue. He raised his thick black eyebrows to force his eyes open. "That moozoo took a lot outta me."

Nicole reached under the narrow table and patted his thigh. "You're a good man," she said. "You should go to bed. It's another big day tomorrow. My nookomis keeps saying this winter is gonna be a rough one."

TWO

They awoke to the rapid, high-pitched buzz of their alarm. Dull red numbers announced that it was 6:30. Hearing nothing from the children's rooms, Nicole hit the snooze button. Evan rolled over, away from her. The light of dawn had yet to creep in through the cracks in the curtain. Sleep was still thick in the room.

The alarm buzzed again and this time Nicole sat up and shifted her feet over the side of the bed. She stood up, reached for her robe in the dark, and slipped it on.

"You got them?" mumbled Evan.

"Yeah, don't worry about it. You had a long day yesterday. Go back to sleep. I'll get them breakfast."

He awoke some time later to the chatter of the children in the kitchen. He heard something about one of their favourite TV shows that he couldn't quite make out.

Satellite must still be out, he thought. *They're usually not talking this much.*

He located some clothing on the floor and pulled on a pair of track pants and a T-shirt. He squinted as he stepped out of the hallway into the kitchen. The sun was now well above the horizon, shining through the big picture window that faced east.

Nangohns's pigtails swayed as she turned her head in his direction. "Hi, Daddy!"

"Mino gizheb," Evan answered. "Good morning, my sweetheart!" He approached the table and kissed her on the forehead. She beamed at him while he turned to greet his son. "Hey bud!" Evan rubbed the boy's short brown hair.

"Good morning, Dad," Maiingan replied. Evan walked into the kitchen, kissed Nicole on the cheek, and poured himself a cup of black coffee.

The morning sun caught the maple and oak trees in front of the house, burnishing them gold and rich brown. The trees and some of the wildlife around them were preparing to sleep while the humans prepared for the great annual test. Evan sometimes envied the trees and black bears that could shut down for the winter.

A sip of the hot, strong coffee snapped him out of his reverie and he walked over to look at his phone that he had left to charge. Nangohns and Maiingan smiled at him from the phone's screen. No notifications or messages. Not even a text, though his phone had been dead the whole afternoon before. He picked it up for a closer look and saw that there were no bars showing in the upper left corner.

"No cell service," he muttered.

"Really?" said Nicole. "I'll go check mine." She walked to

the bedroom and emerged a moment later, peering down at her own phone. "Hmmm, mine's out too."

Cell service outages were common. The cell tower had gone up only a few years before, when the community was finally connected to the wider hydro grid. Even then it only happened because the construction contractors from the South wanted a good signal while they built the massive new hydro dam farther north on the bay. The tower had stayed up after they left, a new luxury for people who lived on the reserve. Many of them hadn't yet developed any sort of serious dependence on the service. An outage didn't evoke any real sense of frustration or panic.

"Whatcha doin' today, Dad?"

His son's voice brought Evan's focus from phone service back to his family. He turned to face the kitchen. "N'gwis, my boy," he said, "I got a lotta work to do. A moose — a moozoo — gave himself to us yesterday."

"You got a moose?!"

"Yep. A big one. It took me a long time to get him out of the bush. That's why I wasn't home when you went to bed last night."

"Cool!"

The boy was eager to join his father on his first hunt but that was still a few years away. Evan first went on an actual hunt with his own father when he was nine, after spending years learning about the land. He had shot his first buck that fall. They didn't offer tobacco when they killed animals to eat back then — Evan only learned about that ceremony years earlier, when an elder took it upon herself to teach him and some of the other young people the old ways.

Maiingan shoved the last spoonful of cereal into his mouth. He dropped the spoon and cupped his small brown hands under the bowl, lifting it to slurp up the last of the milk. Nicole emerged from the bedroom in a pair of jeans and a grey hoodie, her hair gathered in a tight bun. She urged their son to put his bowl in the sink and get dressed for school while Evan cleared the rest of the table. He piled the dirty dishes on the counter, plugged the sink, and turned on the hot water.

As he squeezed the bottle of yellow dish soap into the water, he wondered how long the cellphones would be down. *Shit*, he thought, *I was gonna ask Isaiah to come over and help with the rest of that moose.* He stopped himself and smiled. The landline. It was still what most of the older generation used, and since the cell tower was unreliable, Evan and Nicole kept it around. Evan picked up the house phone, relieved that the familiar dial tone still hummed.

"Can I come hunting too, Daddy?" said Nangohns behind him.

"Eh n'daanis," he replied. "Yes, you can, my girl. But not until you're older."

"Where's the moozoo?"

"Moozoo gojing. It's outside."

"Can I see it?"

"Gaawiin, not yet, my sweetheart. He's not ready."

"Okay."

He took her small hand in his and looked down into her wide brown eyes and smiled. Her pigtails stuck out like antennas on the old TVs. But the little girl's questions often lingered in Evan's mind long after she asked them, and he believed she held the wisdom of countless generations, despite her youth. She was an old soul. He wanted her to question everything. He wanted her to grow up to be strong and intelligent. He wanted her to be a leader.

The morning silence was eerie but soothing. Often, the TV would be on throughout the weekday morning routine, and again on Saturdays for cartoons. Evan hadn't even thought about turning it on, and the kids didn't seem to mind that they ate at the table rather than on the couch. *I dunno what she said to them*, he thought, *but it worked.* Maybe they could keep the TV off in the mornings.

Evan assumed that the satellite reception was still out. Or maybe Nicole just didn't even bother to check. Either way, the kids always listened to her and he appreciated how she guided their children, patiently and with love and respect. He tried to think about how her parenting fit in to the teachings he was learning, but his mind was racing so he ran his fingers over his buzzed hair and let it go.

There had been no satellite TV in the community when Evan was little, just a CBC signal from a tower near the bay that the rabbit ears could pick up as long as there wasn't a storm. But people did have VCRs, and the tapes kept him and his siblings entertained when they were inside. Mostly he remembered playing outside.

Nicole came back with a dressed Maiingan in tow. "Okay, I'm taking the boy to school."

"We'll be here." Evan looked at their daughter, who was still at the table, and she flashed a bright smile. "Let's go wave bye to your brother," he said. He picked her up and they stood in the window to wave as Nicole and Maiingan got in the blue pickup and pulled out of the driveway.

Maiingan was one of only a dozen kids in his class. The community's elementary school was small, with an enrolment of a little more than one hundred, but it was in a new building and the people on the reserve were happy that their kids could finally be educated in a decent facility. Nicole and Evan had gone to school in mouldy prefab makeshift classrooms that had finally, blessedly, crumbled.

There had been lots of infrastructure improvements on the reserve over the last few years, including their connection to the hydro grid. The old diesel generators that had run their lightbulbs and appliances for decades were still around, but they didn't need them anymore. They remained for backup, and the band no longer had to constantly truck in fuel for them. The hydro lines had also opened up a permanent service road that ran some three hundred kilometres south and connected to the main highway. They relied less on the airstrip for supplies and travel and now had the freedom to drive out on their own, theoretically. The weather and lack of maintenance often played havoc with that fine thought, though.

Evan looked down at Nangohns. *This place has changed a lot*, he thought. *It'll be a lot better for you, my little star.*

Once Nicole returned, Evan finished tidying the kids' toys in the living room and poured himself another cup of coffee. He sipped slowly from the blue mug and looked out the kitchen window. *Better get to work*, he thought. "I'm going out to the shed," he called. "Gotta finish up that moose."

It was cold outside, and the scent of the withering leaves on the ground was potent. A fire burned somewhere nearby. Evan instinctively looked to the south for any signs of movement or life. Everything was still except for the sound of an engine in the distance, a four-wheeler, approaching from the heart of the village that lay to the north of his home. Soon the vehicle came into view and he recognized his friend Isaiah North in full rez fall fashion — neon vest over a camouflage jacket. Isaiah pulled into the driveway, parked beside the blue pickup, and turned off the engine. When he stood to dismount, his tall, lean frame towered over the truck's roof. "What's goin' on, bud?"

"Not much, Izzy," Evan replied. "Was just going out to the shed. Got a moozoo yesterday."

"Good. Bull?"

"Yep."

Isaiah took off his cap and ran his right hand through his

short, thick hair as Evan walked down the porch stairs. Side by side, Evan was a head shorter than his friend.

"I figured you musta shot something," Isaiah said. "I didn't hear from you all day. I was gonna text you this morning, but I got no service."

"Yeah, me neither," said Evan, pulling his phone out of his pocket to check again. Still nothing. "I was gonna text you too, but figured you'd just come by anyways."

"Can't keep me away when you got a big ol' bull nearby!" the friend proclaimed, stretching his arms wide.

"Alright then, you can help me finish him off. Maybe I'll let you have the back strips."

"Pffft, ever cheap!"

Evan chuckled and gave Isaiah a punch in the shoulder as he walked past him to the shed.

THREE

The days were growing shorter. But it had been a mostly sunny fall and the unusual run of blue skies had so far kept winter at bay. Deep into the afternoon, it was another vibrant day. Evan grabbed his sunglasses that lay beside his useless cellphone and perched them on top of his mesh fishing hat. He caught a glimpse of his reflection in the television on the wall. It had been off for almost two days now. He thought of how much he had paid for both the phone and the TV on a trip to the city back in the spring, and he was annoyed that he currently could use neither.

"Think it's the weather?" Evan had asked Isaiah while they worked on the moose.

"Doubt it. Probably just bad receivers. We can never have nice things on the rez!"

Evan smiled remembering the conversation. He turned to the kitchen and opened the fridge to grab two large bags of moose meat. Each clear bag contained a large shoulder cut, with the date scrawled on the outside in black marker. He went outside to his truck, opened the door, and threw the meat on the passenger seat. He hoisted himself in and started up his vehicle.

The drive to his parents' place was short. He tuned in to the community radio station, Rez 98.1 on the FM dial. A bluesy song filled the cab. *Well, at least we still got the radio*, he thought. *We may as well be going back in time.* Rez 98 transmitted from a portable outside the band office, and it mostly broadcast generic, preprogrammed playlists interspersed with community announcements and weather updates. The live stuff depended on when Vinny, the resident radio personality, was in the office.

Gravel knocked into the truck's wheel wells as Evan drove through the quiet rez. It was too cold for baseball or fishing but not cold enough for ice at the outdoor rink, so he figured that most of the kids were indoors, playing video games or watching DVDs. He passed the rink on the right, empty and dark under its grey sheet-metal roof. The rink was another recent addition. *If that was here when I was younger*, he thought, *I mighta made something of myself in hockey.*

But in truth, Evan had never really wanted to leave this place. The comfort and familiarity of his community and the pull of the land made him a proud rez lifer. After finishing high school, he'd had no desire to go on to post-secondary education, even to a community college in one of the nearer towns, let alone any of the small northern cities like Gibson or Everton Mills. Job opportunities on the rez were few but neither was the competition stiff, especially in maintenance and infrastructure.

His father, Dan, worked for the roads department, so he started there. Evan had worked part-time at first and spent the rest of his time hunting and fishing.

Evan turned right onto the third road past the rink, then pulled into the fourth driveway on the left. He had checked that they were home before leaving, amused that he had resorted to the landline instead of the usual one-line text to his dad. He parked in front of the bungalow with red vinyl siding and a high basement — the same house he'd grown up in. He got out of his truck and walked around to the back, where he knew his father was tanning a moose hide.

"Careful bent over like that," Evan said as he approached his father. "It ain't good for your back. Plus one of them bulls might see his chance and get his revenge!" He laughed loudly.

Dan kept scraping the thick yellow hide tied to a rectangular stretcher. "Make yourself useful and grab that scraper down there," he said. Evan saw another scraping tool on top of the large blue plastic bin that his father often used for soaking hides. He picked it up and took his place to Dan's right.

They worked silently at first, as they often did. It usually wasn't until a job was done that they spoke. Whether tanning a hide, cleaning a haul of fish from a net, or tackling repairs around their homes, they were business first and fun later. Evan believed that it had taught him about working hard and getting the job done.

Evan dug the fleshing device hard into the softening hide, scraping flesh and fat away from the skin. Dan had been at this since the evening before and was nearly finished. He didn't really need Evan's help, but moments like this were special; it was an intimacy they kept to themselves.

When the hide was completely cleaned, the two men stood back to look at their handiwork — future moccasins, gloves, and pouches. The thick brown hair on the hide still needed to be pulled, so the job wasn't done yet, but it wouldn't take much longer.

Dan turned to Evan. "Smoke break?"

"Yeah, good call."

They each pulled a red rectangular box out of the left pocket of their hunting jackets that were identical except in colour. Almost simultaneously, they each removed a cigarette, lit it, and put the pack and a lighter back in the jacket. Evan inhaled deeply and tipped his head back, exhaling up into the cool November air. Dan sat down on one of the log stools close to the plastic hide containers.

Dan brought the cigarette to his heavy lips. His black moustache tickled the top of the smoke as he took a drag. He looked at the ground between his heavy boots and pushed the smoke out of his nose. Then he looked up at Evan. "So how much meat you got then?"

"Enough." Evan paused. "I got another one yesterday."

"Yeah, that's what Izzy said. He was by here just about an hour ago."

Evan should have known the moccasin telegraph would have been active. He wasn't surprised that his father had already heard the news.

"I brought some for youse guys," he said.

"Better bring it in to your mother then."

They finished their smokes in silence, taking turns looking up from the ground to examine the land around them. Each had nothing to say, and that was fine. They said what they needed to when they needed to.

"'K, I'm gonna take that in to Mom then."

"Yeah, go ahead. I'll start a fire, then we'll finish cleaning that hide."

"Alright."

When Evan walked into the house, the entire main floor

smelled like the moose roast that was in the oven, a familiar and comforting aroma. His mother, Patricia, was sitting at the desk on the far side of the living room. She rapped the black computer mouse loudly on the desktop. "The goddamn internet isn't working!" she announced without turning around. "Come here, Ev. Fix this for me!"

"Okay, just wait then," her son replied. "Where do you want me to put these?" He held up the clear bags of moose meat.

She turned to look and smiled, her cheeks pushing into the bottom of her glasses. "Ever the good son! Just put that on the counter, and I'll take them downstairs to the freezer later. I gotta rearrange the other one your dad just got."

Evan set the meat down on the scarred white countertop in the kitchen. He could navigate this house with his eyes closed, and every step through each room was like muscle memory. The heavy oak dinner table anchored the house, the centre of so much family history. He went back into the living room to assist his mother, walking past the comfortable black leather couch, love seat, and armchair and wishing they had been there when he was a kid. They were all so soft, and they still smelled new.

He stood behind her as she slammed the black mouse again. "What the hell is wrong with this? I gotta check my email!" Evan smirked, knowing that his mom was hooked on online euchre tournaments. There wasn't any money in it but there was international glory, and she liked the idea of playing her favourite game against people from all over the continent.

"How long has yours been out?" he asked.

"Just since yesterday afternoon. I was chatting with your sister online and then it crashed. Then I tried to text her and that didn't work either."

Evan raised his right eyebrow. "Your TV's not working either, eh?"

"No, not since around the same time. I thought all these new dishes and towers and stuff were supposed to be better!"

"Well, I guess it's not all totally reliable all the way up here," he assured her and himself. "All this stuff doesn't go out as much as it used to."

"Yeah, I guess so."

"Now you have more time to make supper. Maybe we'll actually eat on time for once!"

She elbowed him in the gut. "Oh, you shut up," she huffed as she stood up to go to the kitchen.

The truth is, Evan thought, *these things do work better than they used to*. High speed internet access had been in the community for barely a year. It was provided by the band, but connected to servers in the South via satellite. Still, the fact that TV, phone, and internet were all down at once made Evan uneasy.

Metal pots and pans crashed together, and Evan realized he was staring blindly at the computer screen that read *Can't connect to server*. He blinked hard and gave his head a little shake.

"So when are Nic and the kids coming?" Patricia asked from the kitchen.

Evan cleared his throat. "I dunno, I'll go get them in time for supper, I guess. She said she was gonna get the kids to help her make pies when I left."

"Mmmmmm. What kind?"

Evan smiled, picturing his children on chairs across the counter from his wife, watching intently as she opened a can of cherries. "I'm not telling. It's gonna be a surprise."

"Oooooh!" Pat placed a big steel pot of peeled potatoes in the sink. She turned on the tap to fill the pot and grabbed a salt shaker from the top of the stove, shaking salt into the water.

"I'm gonna head back outside," he said.

"Okay then."

Outside, Dan had begun to strip the hide of its fur. It was

usually the easiest step in the process, and he appeared to be making good progress. The dead leaves on the ground rustled around Evan's feet. "About time," Dan said without looking up.

The son took his spot beside his father again. "What you thinking about doing with this one?"

"I dunno, maybe your mom can make something of it." Patricia usually made moccasins and sold them to trading posts and souvenir shops throughout the North. It was good extra money.

They stood quietly again. That comfortable, easy, important silence between a father and a son fell upon them. Evan pulled out his pack of cigarettes once more, and so did Dan. They took long, soothing drags on their smokes, staring into the hide and occasionally into the forested horizon.

Without turning, Dan said, "I had a dream last night." Evan's head turned slowly in his father's direction. "It was night. It was cold, kinda like this time of year. But it was the springtime. I dunno how I could tell because it was so dark, but I just knew that it was.

"I was walking through the bush. I remember I had my shotgun over my shoulder. I had a backpack on too. I dunno why or what was in it." His sentences came out slowly, with a precise rhythm. Evan dragged on his cigarette again, transfixed by his father's unusually candid speech.

"There was this little hill in the distance. I could see it only because it looked like there was something burning on the other side. There was this orange glow. It was pretty weird. It wasn't anyplace I recognized. Nowhere around here, anyways. So I kept walking towards the hill. The light on the other side got brighter. I knew it was a big fire, the closer I got."

Evan couldn't remember the last time his father had spoken so much at once. He wasn't known as a storyteller or a talented orator. *He never talks about dreams*, Evan thought.

Dan continued, "As I went up that hill, I started to see the flames. They were so high. The fire roared, kinda like the rapids down the river. It was popping and cracking real loud. And then I got to the top."

Evan's face tightened and the hair at the back of his neck stood up.

"The whole field on the other side of that hill was on fire. I couldn't see nothing in that field except fire. But it wasn't spreading. Then I looked around and seen a bunch of you guys standing and looking at it. It was you, Cam, Izzy, some of your buddies, and even Terry. There were a bunch more too, but I couldn't tell who they were because they were too far away. You were all spread out, just looking at the fire."

Evan inhaled deeply. His cigarette had burned down to the filter between his fingers, singeing the orange paper.

"Everyone was wearing hunting gear and had their guns in their hands. But no one had any orange on, like right now. And when I looked closer at your face, you looked real skinny. Cam too. And the other guys looked weak. It was pretty weird.

"Then I understood what was going on. We had put the burn on to try to get some moose in. I can't remember the last time we had to do that around here. But everyone in my dream must have been hungry. No one was saying nothing. I looked over at you —" He paused and turned to look at Evan. "You looked at me. You looked scared. And that's when I woke up."

Dan went silent, and Evan stared at his feet. When he looked back to his father's face, Dan's eyes were locked on the bush in the distance.

"Well, maybe if you didn't hunt out them moose this year, we wouldn't have to worry about it," Evan blurted, with a nervous chuckle. "We got a good haul of them anyways." He anxiously watched to see if Dan's hardened, blank face would break.

When the corners of his dad's mouth turned up in a small smile, Evan was relieved.

"You young buggers are the ones hunting them out!" Dan said, as he playfully punched his son in the shoulder. "Shoulda never taught you how to shoot a gun."

They both laughed and turned to go back into the house.

FOUR

Nicole opened her eyes to see daylight punching through the narrow gap in the thick blue curtains. It created a rectangular halo in an otherwise dark and cold bedroom. The frigid air made her nose numb. Suddenly, she was wide awake, well-rested but uneasy.

She looked over to the alarm clock and noticed that its red glow was gone. Evan was still asleep beside her. She cast aside the covers and stood up, putting on her thick robe over her T-shirt and pyjama pants. It was Friday, and she was certain Maiingan would be late for school. She stepped into her deerskin moccasins by the door. The soft rabbit fur of the lining caressed the tender skin between her toes, putting her momentarily at ease.

The chill was harsher out in the hallway. She peeked quickly into the kids' rooms and saw that both were still sleeping, curled in their thick blankets decorated with their favourite cartoon characters. *Maybe it's earlier than I thought.* The battery-powered clock on the far wall of the kitchen indicated it was just after 7:30 a.m. Not too late for school, but barely early enough to get everyone up and ready for the day.

The cold upstairs meant the wood stove in the basement was out. And with the electricity now off too, the baseboard heaters hadn't kicked in to compensate for the dead fire. Sometimes they would forget to feed the fire before bed, knowing that if it died down, the electric heat would kick in. But power outages happened regularly enough to remind them to stay on top of it.

"Jesus, it's freezing in here!" she heard Evan say behind her. He walked out into the bright kitchen, wearing a black tracksuit and thick wool socks.

"Yeah, power's out," Nicole replied.

"Really?"

Noticing the surprised uptick in his voice, she tried to reassure both of them. "Yeah, we just forgot to put more wood in the stove," she said. "Remember when this happened last winter?"

His shoulders relaxed slightly. "Oh yeah, eh," he said. "Guess I better go down and start that up again." He scratched his head. "Hopefully the power comes back on soon, or it's just gonna be cereal and cold bread for breakfast!"

Like most of the homes that had been built or brought in pre-fabricated in the last decade, theirs relied heavily on electric appliances. When Evan was a child, his home's stove and fridge had been fuelled by propane — handy in case the diesel delivery didn't come through. With a lighter demand and smaller storage tanks, propane didn't have to be trucked in as regularly.

But the hydro lines from the massive dam to the east now

powered homes here, and there were plans to decommission the band's diesel generators and sell them. There was still diesel in them for contingencies, but the upcoming winter was to be the last that the band paid for trucks to bring in the fuel.

The narrow basement windows gave Evan just enough light to start another fire in the big metal box on the far side of the cold, damp room. Upstairs, Nicole roused the children to get their day started. If the power didn't come back on within the next hour, school would likely be cancelled. She began thinking of activities to keep them occupied if that was the case.

As she watched the kids saunter into the kitchen, Nicole caught sight of the phone on the wall. Out of curiosity, she picked the handset off its holster and brought it to her ear. The cold plastic chilled her earlobe. She heard nothing. She had a moment of quick panic but stifled it to focus on feeding the children.

They were sitting at the table, eating peanut butter and strawberry jam sandwiches when Evan came back upstairs twenty minutes later. The air inside slowly warmed and the now-familiar silence made for a quiet, comfortable space in the home. Nicole decided to wait until after breakfast to tell Evan about the dead phone.

There was a knock at the front door, and when Evan stood up from the table to look, he could see Nicole's older cousin Tammy standing on the porch. She smiled and waved, then opened the door and walked in. She was wearing a heavy burgundy coat that made crinkling sounds as she closed the door behind her. "Aaniin!" she called out. Her black hair was tied back in a tight bun that seemed to pull her smile even wider.

"Aaniin!" Evan replied. "Aaniish na? What's up?"

"Oh, just making the rounds," she said. Her voice was always louder than anyone else in Nicole's family. It came in handy as the school's receptionist. "I see the power's out over here too?"

"Yeah, musta gone out in the night sometime. We slept in."

"I think everyone did."

"We let the furnace go out too. I just got it back going. I guess we're getting too used to hydro."

"I was gonna say, I'm pretty sure I can still see my breath in here!" She exhaled slowly through her mouth and tugged at the collar of her jacket. "Anyway, I came by to let youse know that there's no school today. Phones and internet aren't working, and we were too lazy to get the good old-fashioned smoke signals going today!" She followed that with big laughter.

Evan shot a puzzled glance at Nicole, who was still in the kitchen. "Landlines aren't working either?" She grimaced and shook her head. He looked to the floor and pushed that worry out of his mind before turning his attention back to Tammy.

"If you're the moccasin telegraph, where's your moccasins then?" Evan looked down at the high brown leather boots she'd bought at a mall on a trip down to Gibson. "Musta been a handsome moose you shot!" He laughed and Tammy scoffed.

"Anyways," she said, "hopefully we'll get the power back on this weekend and have school on Monday. I'll let ya know."

Evan nodded. "It's kinda weird to have everything out. When's the last time we had no satellite, phones, or hydro?"

"I dunno. Couldn't have been that long ago. Last year maybe," said Evan.

"You sure? I don't remember."

"If not last year, then definitely the year before. Remember how nothing really worked all the time when they first put up that tower and started bringing in those lines?"

"Yeah, I guess so, eh."

"Don't worry about it. Geez, back in our day we never had none of this shit!" Tammy was fifteen years older than Evan and Nicole. "You guys should count your lucky stars."

It was true. He had spent most of his life without cell service and satellite TV, and his parents had grown up without power at all.

"You're right," he muttered. "Thanks for coming by and letting us know."

Nicole walked over to the door with Nangohns trailing behind and Tammy's face lit up as the little girl ran into her arms. "Oh good morning, my little star!" She bounced the smiling girl in her arms. "Well, guess I should get going. Youse wanna come over for some poker tomorrow night? We'll be around. Hopefully the lights will be back on!"

"Okay, cool, miigwech," said Nicole.

"Alright then, you know where to find us." Tammy put Nangohns down and left.

Evan felt the cold air sneak inside as the door closed. Soon the temperature outside would drop further and the first big snowfall loomed. It was a good time to split more wood for the furnace.

Outside, the air was dry and cold. A breeze bit his high, broad cheeks. The clear sky seemed unthreatening but there would be a storm soon. There always was. That's when his job would really get busy, clearing snow from roads and driveways with the band's snowploughs. Evan's job responsibilities changed season to season. Springtime usually meant he was out on the roads, patching holes and laying gravel on asphalt that had washed away in the runoff. In the summer, he monitored the water quality at the treatment plant. By fall, he made home visits to make sure pipes, cisterns, and septic tanks were ready for winter. And when the snow fell, he was one of the ploughmen.

In the backyard stood five firm walls of wood piled neatly into ten cords waiting to be split. Gathering wood was a year-round process on the rez. People went into the bush to cut down spruce, oak, and maple to bring home for their own use or to sell. The band employed its own crew to provide wood for the elderly and others who needed help, and Evan brought any leftover wood home whenever he could.

He worked a few logs free from the top of the nearest stack and shoved them to the ground. He tipped the closest one upright and brought the axe up to his waist to begin his swing, his left hand closest to the butt of the handle and his right by the blade. He raised it high over his head and brought his hands together as he dropped the axe down, splitting the log with a loud crack that echoed into the field behind his home.

"Whoa, good swing, pipes!" Evan recognized his younger brother's voice behind him. He looked over his shoulder to see a wide grin baring stained yellow teeth. Cam's ball cap was pulled tightly over his forehead, concealing his eyes and causing his thick, greasy black hair to protrude in all directions.

"Oh, good, just in time to help!" Evan replied.

"Yeah, maybe if you give me a smoke," said Cam.

"We'll see. So what are you up to?"

"Nothin', man. Fuckin' bored. Can't do nothin' without no power."

Cam didn't have a job. He worked occasionally when the trees had to be cleared for the power lines or when a road crew was needed, but otherwise he spent his time playing video games at the apartment he shared with his girlfriend, Sydney, and their son, Jordan. They lived in the cluster of duplex buildings originally built for hydro workers, but after the men from the South left, the housing was made available to band members. It was temporary housing for the southerners but, like so much on the rez, it stayed up and got used.

"Good. About time you got up off your ass," Evan poked.

"Fuck off. When's the power supposed to come back on?" he asked.

"No idea. We froze our asses off last night because I let the furnace go out. That's why I'm chopping more wood now, just in case."

"Yeah, it was pretty chilly in our place too. Good thing Izzy and those guys came around early this morning to start ours."

"Do you guys have enough wood to keep it going?" Evan asked.

"Yeah, I think so. They left some more for us."

"You should know how to start that yourself anyways."

"Meh, whatever."

Only two years separated the brothers, but somehow Evan had landed on his feet in adulthood while Cam hadn't yet. When Evan had been out on the land learning real survival skills with his father and uncles as a teenager, Cam had chosen to stay behind, learning simulated ones in video games.

"Well, be a good uncle for your niece and nephew anyway, and go grab that axe by that pile."

Cam grumblingly obliged and the two split logs as the sun moved across the sky. Somewhere out on the road, a pack of dogs yelped and barked at something in the bush. They knew the storm was coming soon too.

FIVE

Three hard knocks woke Nicole and Evan. She groaned, and he turned over as three more thuds vibrated through the house. "What the hell is that?" she mumbled.

Evan groaned. "I'll go check."

He got out of bed in his T-shirt and boxer shorts in the grey predawn light.

At the door, he recognized the familiar silhouette of Isaiah, who smiled mischievously at Evan's sleep-rumpled state and walked in.

"I woulda said whatever happened to calling," Evan grumbled, "but I remembered the phones are out."

"Yeah, all moccasin telegraph all the time these days," Isaiah replied. Evan was already tired of this joke. Izzy fell into the armchair beside the door without taking off his heavy red parka, grey toque, or boots.

"What's going on?"

"Terry wants everyone in public works over at the band office right away. He pounded at my door just about fifteen minutes ago. My job was to round you up."

"It's Saturday, damn it!"

"Yeah, well, he says it's an emergency. He's talking about firing up the generator. No one knows what's going on with the hydro."

The chief calling an emergency meeting on a Saturday morning was serious. Evan snapped awake. "Alright, lemme go get dressed," he said. "What's it like outside?"

"Gettin' colder."

"Shit."

Evan quickly returned to the bedroom, where Nicole lay awake in the warm, uneasy darkness. "What's Izzy want?"

"Gotta go to work," he replied, as he picked up the jeans from the floor and pulled them on.

"What's going on?"

"Not totally sure, but Izzy says Terry wants everyone in public works over at the shop. Guess he wants to turn the generator on."

"That's good. The food in the fridge might start to go bad without the power."

"Yeah, and it'd be good to put the kids in front of a movie for a break," he said with a laugh.

He leaned in to kiss his partner and walked back to the front door, where his outside clothes hung on the hook.

Once he was dressed, Evan and Isaiah stepped outside into the cold. A faint pink glow in the east hinted at the sunrise. *I guess it's not that early*, Evan thought.

They climbed into Isaiah's idling truck, and Evan appreciated the warmth of the cab. Isaiah turned up the country music on his truck's stereo and backed out onto the road.

"First you wake me up to work on a Saturday, then you make me listen to this shit?" Evan said.

"Shut the hell up," his friend shot back. "This music is about real pain and struggle. It's our people's music."

Evan rolled his eyes and looked out the window, willing to let the music be a distraction from his worries. He loved his friend like a brother. They'd been through almost everything together — hunts, hardships, and heartaches — but he couldn't stand Isaiah's taste in music.

Each house the truck passed was dark. There wouldn't be much activity in these homes this early on a Saturday anyway, but every unlit window was hard to ignore.

As the late fall sun began to peek over the horizon, its low angle cast tiny shadows behind the bigger chunks of gravel spread across the route. The shallow streams in the deep ditches on either side were frozen solid.

The truck rolled through the village to the outskirts on the other side of town. Black spruce trees closed in around them as they approached the generating station by the shop. The reverberating echo of a slide guitar faded slowly as Isaiah lined his truck up with the six other pickup trucks in front of the high brick building. He smiled as he parked, no doubt amused that he had made Evan endure another country song.

Terry Meegis, the chief, stood near the green front door with Evan's father, having a smoke. Evan wasn't surprised to see Dan there. He was head of the band's public works department and would be instrumental in any decisions that needed to be made.

Evan and Isaiah got out of the truck and approached the two older men. The huge white diesel tanks that loomed over the shop were stained a deep orange by the rising sun. The sky above was brightening into a more comforting azure.

"Mino gizheb niniwag. Aaniish na?" said Terry.

"Morning," they replied. Evan noticed dark circles under Terry's eyes. He was only a couple of years older than Dan, but it was obvious that he wasn't getting much sleep recently. The chief took a drag from his cigarette and ran a hand through his coarse hair. His short hairstyle caused his wiry hair to puff out around his ears and he looked just as he had for as long as Evan could remember, a reassuring constant in band life.

The chief wasted no time. "We don't know what's going on with the power. Or the cellphones or the TV." He looked at the two young men. Dan had already been briefed, so he stood slightly out of the circle, looking to the sunrise.

"We have no communication with anyone from Hydro," he continued. "The satellite phone's not working, and we can't pick up anything on the other end of the old shortwave radio. Before people start getting worried or acting crazy, we're gonna fire up the generators. We'll at least be able to hold them over through the weekend and into next week if we need to."

Evan and Isaiah nodded, then looked at each other cautiously. Terry noticed. "Don't shit your pants," he said. "We've dealt with this before. These things go out all the time. It's just been a while since all of them were down at the same time. We'll get the lights on for the weekend and regroup Monday."

Then Dan took over. "Tyler, JC, and a couple of the other boys are in there right now," he said, gesturing over his shoulder into the building. "They're getting the generators ready to fire up. We were scheduled to test them next week anyways. This is a good chance to do a run-through."

Evan breathed out in relief, a bit embarrassed he'd been so worried.

"Joanne is down at the band office getting ready to print

off notices," Terry continued. Tyler's mom was one of the band administrators. In a small community, family members worked together all the time. Terry and Dan had been friends since childhood, and JC Meegis, who was inside running tests, was Terry's son.

"We're going to tell people that we've turned the generators on so no one's food goes bad and so they can get their houses warm. If the power doesn't come back over the weekend, we're gonna have a community meeting Monday afternoon at the band office. I brought you guys here because I thought we needed more maintenance done inside before these machines fire up. But it looks like it's under control."

The loud cranking of an engine echoed off the walls of the shop and one of the generators roared into operation.

"So we just need you two to deliver the flyers," said Terry.

"Fuck, really?" said Isaiah.

"What's your problem?"

"I don't wanna go door to door on a Saturday morning."

"You just have to drop them off, dumbass. The power's gonna be on, so it's not like anyone will be demanding answers from you."

Evan chuckled.

"What's so funny, Tweedle Dum?" prodded the chief.

"Nothing."

"Okay then, get your asses to work! We'll update you later."

Evan looked at his father, and Dan gave him an easy smile back.

The sun was up and shining through the dust on the windshield as they drove back east into the heart of the community to pick up the notices from the band office. Songs of heartache and liquor blared again inside the cab. The fingers of Isaiah's left hand were curling into different positions as it rested on the steering wheel.

"Don't tell me you're actually learning this shit?"

"Huh?" Isaiah looked to Evan then down at his fingers, positioned in a C chord on an air guitar. "Oh, yeah, I was just playing along in my mind."

"What happened to your taste, man? You used to play the good stuff." Evan shook his head.

Isaiah sang along in a nasally twang, as Evan sat back and thought fondly of the heavy metal they'd listened to as teens.

They rolled to a stop in front of the green single-storey building that housed the band office, the school, and the health centre. Evan stepped out of the truck to run in and get the flyers. He pulled the glass front doors open to find Joanne Birch waiting for him at her desk.

"Hold on, just printing them off now," she said, without looking up from the computer screen. "I guess everything's working up there?" Her brown hair fell in two tight braids that draped over her black hoodie emblazoned with the rez logo — an outline of three spruce trees on the white, yellow, red, and black background of the four directions circle.

"Seems to be," he replied. "Everything here working?"

"The computer and the lights are on. All systems go, I guess."

"When's the last time the lights were on in here on a Saturday?"

"Beats me, I ain't never worked on a Saturday. It's the band office!"

They chortled and Evan gazed out over the spacious lobby as he waited. Its walls were lined with local art and a birchbark canoe hung from the beams below the skylight.

"You guys staying warm at home?" Evan asked.

"Yeah, Tyler had the furnace going pretty good. Didn't even notice the power was off until it was time to make breakfast yesterday." Tyler, who worked with Evan and Isaiah, was a few years younger than they and still lived at home.

"Right on. I slacked and let ours burn out."

"What kinda Nishnaab are you?"

"I know. The kids didn't seem to mind though."

"Well, good thing you can at least put some videos on the TV now. I bet their patience is wearing thin. You're lucky you got a good kwe at home to raise them right."

Evan nodded. His heart fluttered.

Joanne rolled over to the printer, then back over to him, and handed over the stack of sheets. "Alright, here ya go. Have fun!"

As he stepped outside, Evan looked down at the flyer he was to distribute.

NOTICE

COMMUNITY-WIDE POWER OUTAGE

EMERGENCY POWER GENERATION IN EFFECT UNTIL FURTHER NOTICE
PLEASE CONSERVE ENERGY WHERE POSSIBLE
USE WOOD STOVES AND FURNACES AS PRIMARY HEAT SOURCES
SAFELY STORE FOOD
NEXT UPDATE MONDAY
HAVE A GOOD WEEKEND

MIIGWECH,
CHIEF AND COUNCIL

SIX

It was dark by the time Evan and Nicole dropped the children off at Dan and Patricia's. Inside, only the living room lights were on. Maiingan and Nangohns ran to their grandparents with open arms even before taking off their winter jackets.

"Ah, n'nohnshehnyag!" said Patricia. "My little sweethearts, come to your nookomis."

"Thanks for taking them," said Nicole.

"You deserve a night off," Patricia responded. "Go relax."

They waved at their children, who waved back, jumping up and down at the prospect of a night with their grandparents.

"That used to be hard," said Nicole, as she walked down the front stairs, "but some nights, it's pretty easy." Evan laughed.

The roads were dark — the council had decided against turning on the community's few street lights — but the homes scattered along the route all now had some light pouring out into the evening. As he drove to Tammy's place, Evan noted which homes were obeying the band's request to limit power use.

"Shit, look at Vinny's place," he said. "He's got every fuckin' light in his place on!"

Vinny Jones's two-storey home was unusual in this community of bungalows with raised basements. He'd been able to afford it because he worked in the mines to the west. Tonight his house stood out even more as it blazed with light.

"He's probably got his stereo right cranked too," added Nicole. "He's gotta be having a party down in his basement."

"When the shit really hits the fan, what are people like him gonna do?"

"What do you mean?"

"Ah nothing. I'll go talk to him tomorrow."

"Yeah, talk some sense into him."

Most of the other houses had only a couple of lights on, either in the living room or kitchen. Many of the family dwellings here were identical, trucked in on the ice road one half at a time and fastened together. It was easy for Evan and Nicole to pinpoint which light was on in which room. The older homes, some crumbling and facing demolition, were harder to figure out.

They pulled in at a house that looked much like their own. The living room was dark, but they could see activity under the dull kitchen light of Tammy's home. Evan knocked and opened the door without waiting for a response.

"Biindigeg!" bellowed Tammy's husband, Will. "Let's get this game on the go!" They both heard the slowness in his voice.

"Hold your horses!" teased Nicole as she reached down to untie her boots. Evan threw his leather jacket on the chair, and they joined Tammy and Will at the table.

Tammy sat on the near side, twisting around to rest her arm on the chair so she could greet them. Her black hair hung smoothly over her loose navy blue blouse. Across from her, Will held his arms outstretched in a comfortable welcome, Metallica's *Master of Puppets* album stretched across the T-shirt that covered his middle-aged gut. At the centre of the table, a large plastic bottle of rye and another of rum sat surrounded by several big bottles of Coke and ginger ale.

It was supposed to be a dry community. Alcohol had been banished by the band council nearly two decades ago after a snarl of tragedies. Young people had been committing suicide at horrifying rates in the years leading up to the ban, most abetted by alcohol or drugs or gas or other solvents. And for decades, despairing men had gotten drunk and beaten their partners and children, feeding a cycle of abuse that continued when those kids grew up. It became so normal that everyone forgot about the root of this turmoil: their forced displacement from their homelands and the violent erasure of their culture, language, and ceremonies.

But sixteen-year-old Justin Meegis was the breaking point. The teenager had been drinking with friends, and in his stupor stabbed his grandmother over what should have been a minor argument. She died, and so did he after turning the knife on himself. The only logical recourse for the community leadership was to ban alcohol. Almost twenty years later, the regulation was seldom enforced, and alcohol was smuggled in and stockpiled in homes, especially for nights like these.

"Ev, can you grab some ice?" asked Tammy. Evan grabbed the white plastic tray from the freezer and dumped the cubes into a waiting plastic bowl.

He sat down and generously poured rye into the plastic cup in front of him, adding ice and ginger ale. Nicole mixed rum and Coke. Like many people in the community who still drank, they didn't talk about it. It was easier to ignore all the sadness and despair that had come to their families because of alcohol if they just pushed it out of their minds. They indulged to have fun, relax, and forget.

"So, anyone out there following chief and council's wishes?" Tammy asked.

"Yeah, most people," said Evan. "Others, not so much."

"Like who?"

"You can probably figure it out if you think about it."

"Let's just say the people who usually don't have to worry about their bills are carrying on like that," added Nicole.

A deck of cards lay idle at the corner of the table for the remainder of the night. Instead, the two couples sat for hours, refilling their cups and getting up only to use the bathroom. The conversation meandered from hunting and the weather to rez politics and the local gossip.

Eventually Will passed out at the table, and Nicole manoeuvred Evan to bed in the spare room. They were both too drunk to drive home and the kids were sleeping over at their grandparents' anyway.

Waking up the next morning to a still house with the pungent aroma of stale cigarette smoke hanging in the air, Evan felt his usual conflicted morning-after emotions of guilt and defiance. He and Nicole got up quietly and went to pick up the kids. They rode in silence, both looking straight into the bare gravel road before them.

SEVEN

The wind picked up in the early afternoon. Dark clouds rolled in right after. Flurries soon blew around and settled on the ground, speckling the dead leaves and the dirt roads with white flakes that clustered in small, light piles. The howl of the wind kept almost everyone indoors. As the sky grew darker with the increasing snow, families turned their attention to creating comfort in the bright, warm confines of their homes.

Everyone knew a blizzard was imminent. It was usual this time of year. But the radio and online weather reports were silent and no one was sure exactly when the weather would hit.

But here it came, coating roofs, stairs, driveways, and roads with a blanket of snow that seemed to thicken with each blink of the eyes. Evening seemed to creep in quickly. Men and women scurried outside to shovel driveways, salt stairs, and haul wood. Dogs huddled in their shelters and under porches. Snow squeezed the remaining birds out of the fall sky.

The temperature drop and the building wind bit at cheeks and stung eyes and nostrils. Each breath chilled, making survival chores harder. Sweat soaked toques and froze in eyebrows. Hands cramped around shovel handles as fingers grew numb.

The only vehicles to brave the roads were the trucks of the band's employees. A major snowfall meant they were immediately on the clock, clearing snow from the dirt and gravel routes on the rez. Each drove on his own to the shop where the ploughs, trucks, and salters were parked. They rolled them out in careful succession, relying on their customary choreography to keep the roads clear. If the blizzard didn't let up, it was a routine they'd be repeating into the night.

Maiingan looked out the window, his small hands holding on to the wooden sill so he could hike himself up onto tiptoes. He was barely tall enough to peer into the darkness. He saw blurry white headlights coming from the left through the thick blowing snow. "Mommy, is that Daddy?"

"Maybe, my son," Nicole answered, not looking up from the book she was reading to Nangohns. "Wave anyway. Even if it's not him, the other guys would be happy to see you."

The boy waved and smiled widely even though his small head in the large picture window would be barely visible from the road. He continued flapping his hands until the pickup truck with the blade attached to the front bumper was well out of sight.

The smell of bannock wafted through the house, enriching the aroma of the moose stew simmering on the stovetop. It was comfort food, but it was also fuel in harsh winter weather. Nicole had offered to make it for the guys working tonight for whenever they needed a rest and a meal. Evan had spread the word, and the crew would likely start taking up the offer in the coming hours.

Despite the hardship and tragedy that made up a significant part of this First Nation's legacy, the Anishinaabe spirit of community generally prevailed. There was no panic on the night of this first blizzard, although there had been confusion in the days leading up to it. Survival had always been an integral part of their culture. It was their history. The skills they needed to persevere in this northern terrain, far from their original homeland farther south, were proud knowledge held close through the decades of imposed adversity. They were handed down to those in the next generation willing to learn. Each winter marked another milestone.

Nicole closed the children's book, *Jidmoo Miinwaa Goongwaas*, and kissed the top of Nangohns's head. "There you go, my little star," she said, switching from the Anishinaabemowin in the book to English. "Now you know about the squirrel and the chipmunk. You two stay put, I'll be right back up."

She got up from the couch and walked down to the basement to put more wood in the stove. "Everything will be okay, my loves," she said into the dark silence.

EiGHT

Fluorescent lights buzzed over Terry Meegis and the band councillors, who sat at two grey plastic tables at the front of the gymnasium, the centrepiece of the community complex and the biggest gathering space on the rez. Three hundred chairs were lined neatly but only about fifty of them were occupied.

Terry turned to his cousin Walter. "Jesus, where the hell is everyone?"

"Shoulda promised proper food." Walter looked like a taller, younger version of the chief but with long hair.

"How the hell we gonna cook for this many people? We're on the auxiliary generator power already. Besides, we could be looking at food rationing." Terry ran his fingers through his hair and sighed loudly.

"Don't worry about it, Terry," Candace North said. "They'll show up. It's harder to get around with all that snow, especially for the people who have to walk here." She flashed a sweet smile that pushed her cheeks up into her wide-set eyes. Short and heavyset, she was Isaiah's mother and the "auntie" of the council who was most often the voice of reason during meeting disputes. "Let's give them another half hour or so. It looks like the coffee and cookies are holding them over," she reassured, gesturing at the few dozen in the crowd. "Go have a smoke."

Terry took her suggestion and walked outside. The remaining councillors stayed, socializing with band members as they trickled in.

Earlier that morning, after Evan had returned his plough to the yard, he had adjusted the breaker switches on the power panel to provide lights to the main entrance and to the gym. He had filled the diesel furnace with enough fuel to heat the space where the community was to gather later in the day. Now he sat nearby in case they needed him for anything else.

"Just gotta wait now, I guess," Candace said to him.

Evan adjusted the beak of his blue ball cap and looked down at his feet before asking, "So what's going on, anyway?"

She sighed. "We're not really sure yet. Terry's gonna ask everyone just to sit tight while we wait for communication to come back and we hear what's going on with the systems down south."

The chairs filled steadily, and finally about a hundred people sat chatting in their winter gear while children chased each other down the aisle and along the painted sidelines on the floor. Evan saw his parents, his older sister Sarah, and her son Ziigwan stroll in. He smiled at them, and the little boy, just a little older than his own son, waved. He noted that Cam was not with them.

Back at the table, Terry scanned the gym. Relatives, friends, acquaintances, and political enemies sat before them. Governing a community this size, he and the council sometimes had to make decisions that not everyone liked. Some nodded or smiled at him. Others met his gaze without expression. The weathered faces of the dozen or so elders in the crowd analyzed his body language with their chins held high. He nodded at one in particular, Aileen Jones, and she nodded back. He cleared his throat and stood.

"Boozhoo, mino shkwaa naagweg kina wiya," he began. "Good afternoon, everybody. Chi-miigwech for coming down here today. As you all know, we've been having some problems with power and satellite connections, so we're here to give you an update. First though, I'd like to call up our elder Aileen to start this meeting with a smudge and a prayer."

That was Evan's cue, and he walked over to Aileen. She was in her late eighties, one of the oldest of their community, and she had difficulty getting around, so Evan offered his arm to help her up. She looked up at him with eyes so dark the pupils were hard to distinguish from the irises. She smiled her sweet slow smile that rippled the lines of her face. Her thin white hair draped the back of her neck loosely, and she mouthed a faint miigwech as she pulled herself to stand. She picked up the medicine bundle on the chair beside her and handed it to Evan.

Evan reached into the cloth bag, sewn with white, yellow, red, and black material. He felt around for the large abalone shell he knew was inside and pulled it out. The iridescent interior was smooth and gleamed with a swath of subtle pinks and blues. He held the shell upright, its rough exterior nestled in his hand while Aileen's reached into the medicine bag. Evan could smell the sage before she even grabbed it. The entire gym was silent.

Aileen pulled out the sticks of sage and motioned for Evan to hold the shell in front of her. She began breaking them into smaller pieces and piled them neatly in the basin of the shell. She wiped the smaller leaves that stuck to her fingers and palms onto the rest of the medicine. It was important to get it all. The sharp herbal aroma soothed Evan. Next Aileen reached for a box of matches and a fan of eagle feathers that she handed to Evan.

Her wrinkled hands trembled as she pushed open the cardboard box for a match. Her fingers rattled among the matchsticks, and Evan worried she wouldn't be able to pinch one free. But she did and brought the red head of the match swiftly to the coarse side of the box. The loud pop of combustion resounded through the first rows of gym, and the sulphur smell briefly wiped out the sage's scent.

Aileen brought the flickering orange light under the carefully piled sage in the shell, and the medicine caught fire. She let it burn for a few seconds before blowing it out. Thick grey smoke billowed from the shell in Evan's hand, and the unmistakable calming smell of smudge slowly dispersed through the gym. Aileen shook out the match and placed it carefully in the shell. The elder moved through the ceremony as if this were muscle memory passed to her through countless generations.

"Aambe," Aileen said, motioning towards her torso with both of her hands.

Evan carefully waved the feathers across the burning sage, moving more smoke through the room. Aileen cupped her hands over the smudge and started to guide it over her body. She washed it over her head, up and down her arms, down her torso, her legs, and then turned so Evan could smudge her back and shoulders.

Many in the crowd watched intently, awaiting their turn. Others were skeptical, and a smaller few took offence to the ritual, though it was an integral part of Anishinaabe spirituality. It represented a cleansing of the spirit, and the ceremony was believed to clear the air of negativity. It had become protocol to open any community event or council meeting with a smudge.

This protocol had once been forbidden, outlawed by the government and shunned by the church. When the ancestors of these Anishinaabe people were forced to settle in this unfamiliar land, distant from their traditional home near the Great Lakes, their culture withered under the pressure of the incomers' Christianity. The white authorities displaced them far to the north to make way for towns and cities.

But people like Aileen, her parents, and a few others had kept the old ways alive in secret. They whispered the stories and the language in each other's ears, even when they were stolen from their families to endure forced and often violent assimilation at church-run residential schools far away from their homes. They had held out hope that one day their beautiful ways would be able to reemerge and flourish once again.

"Okay," Aileen spoke softly to Evan, "your turn." He handed her the shell and the fan and dipped his hands into the smoke to bring it close to himself. He turned so that his back was to her, and let her disperse the medicine up and down his body. From behind him, she tapped each of his shoulders gently with the fan, and he turned back to face her and took the medicine from her hands. He walked clockwise around the gym, fanning the shell to push the smoke into the air and towards the seated townspeople. He then took a spot over to one side of the council table where people who wanted to smudge could line up.

Aileen turned to the crowd and spoke. "Boozhoo, Zhaawshgogiiizhgokwe n'dizhnakaaz," she said. "Wawashkesh n'dodem." After introducing herself in Anishinaabemowin, she addressed the crowd in English. "Good afternoon, my relatives." Her quiet, authoritative voice echoed through the large room. "Thank you all for coming here today." As an elder, she had the full attention of everyone in the room. Any eyes that might have rolled during the smudge were nonetheless now fixed on her. She was everyone's auntie, even if they weren't related by blood.

"Winter is here," she continued. "Maybe it came a little earlier than we all expected. It's the time when the trees go to sleep. The bears go to sleep. We all rest. And then we will be reborn in the spring. But it's important to make sure we're ready. Now is the time to help your relatives prepare their winter homes. Make sure they have enough food. Enough wood. Enough medicine to make it through the dark season."

Heads nodded in the crowd. Evan tried to read the faces, people no doubt thinking of their own winter inventory and what they would need. Some looked slightly panicked.

"So I'm going to offer a prayer," she smiled. "I'm gonna ask the Great Spirit to take care of us this winter. We're gonna need it." She smiled reassuringly and began to speak in her first language once again, introducing herself once more in Anishinaabemowin, and then giving thanks for health and all the other gifts from the Creator.

Aileen finished with a strong miigwech, and a smattering of responses rolled through the audience as they thanked the elder for opening the meeting. Candace helped her back to her chair while Evan finished smudging the last few people lined up in front of him.

That was Terry's cue. He cleared his throat, wiped his palms on the thighs of his jeans, and stood up. He thanked Aileen for the prayer, and Evan for the smudge. He then thanked everyone who showed up to the all-members meeting.

"As you all know by now," he started, "we're having some

issues with the infrastructure here in the community. If you didn't know, you must be living under a rock." The feeble joke got a chuckle out of some people, and he relaxed a bit. He pushed it. "Anyone who's still living under a rock is buried under three feet of snow by now!" Louder laughter followed. A hint of tension lingered in some stoic faces, but most of it had dissipated.

His voice became more serious. "Last Wednesday, our satellite service went out. That knocked out TV and internet. Most of you noticed. We got a lot of visitors down here at the band office that day. Here we just thought you were all coming to wish Walter a happy birthday," he giggled and looked down at his cousin, and the crowd chuckled again. "These things happen, so we gave it a day. Sometime in there, the phone lines went down for some reason too. When all those things still weren't working on Thursday, we tried to call our service provider down in Gibson with our off-grid sat phone. But that wasn't working either. We figured we'd wait another day just to see if it came on.

"Then sometime overnight Thursday, the power went out. It's the first time we've lost power like that since we connected to the grid three years ago. We sent our guys to check the nearest transformers. They looked fine but they're dead. There's nothing coming in from the dam. And because we have no communication, we've had no updates."

Parkas rustled as people whispered to neighbours and family. From their place at the front of the room, Terry and the councillors could see the anxiety building in the gym.

"Don't worry, we're confident it'll come back on," he quickly uttered. "They spent a hundred million dollars getting this line to us. The longer we go without power, the worse it'll look on the province. So you can be sure there are people down in the big smoke and at the dam working on this right now. We just don't know exactly what the problem is yet."

The rest of the councillors sat looking out at their relatives and friends. Each attempted to appear confident in the uneasy confusion.

"On Saturday, we turned on the generators so you could put the lights and heat back on," Terry reminded them. "We wanted to give you a chance to keep working on whatever you still needed to do before winter. Stuff like arranging your food in your freezers and bringing wood inside. Looks like we did that just in time too. We're keeping the generators on for the time being, but we still need you to conserve energy. Only turn on lights in the room you're in. Don't use your electric oven if you don't have to. If you're gonna watch DVDs, please do it sparingly.

"It's been a long time since the generators ran all winter. The diesel tanks are only half full. We're supposed to get some new shipments in once the service road is iced over for the truckers. We ordered maintenance supplies last month and that delivery is supposed to happen sometime in the next couple weeks. Same time as the next food truckload for the Northern. But hopefully by then, we'll be back on the grid."

"What the fuck, Terry?" a voice shouted from the back. Evan's much older cousin Mark angrily pulled his toque off his head and stood up. "So we just gotta wait around and hope this shit returns to normal?"

"We're just asking you to be patient, Mark," the chief replied. The lights shimmered off Mark's scalp that showed through his thinning brown hair. "The plans are in place. The generators are running. That's what they're there for. Emergencies. They're doing what they're supposed to right now."

A soft murmur emanated from the crowd. Evan couldn't tell if they were appeased or confused, or both.

"So that's why we want you to conserve," Terry continued. "At regular usage, we estimate that we'll run out of diesel by

February. We don't think that'll happen anyway. But to be on the safe side, don't use too much power."

The crowd's restlessness grew. They had come for answers and were getting very few, only directions and orders. *He's losing them*, thought Evan.

"So, because of that," Terry explained, "the school and the band office will be closed for the rest of the week. We'll do our part here too. There will be rotating staff to help with any problems. Public works is on duty all week. Until phone service is back, you'll just have to come down here and ask if you need or want to know something. In the meantime, keep your wood stoves and furnaces going. We want you to stay warm. We also don't want your pipes to freeze."

Terry wrapped up and Walter took over, explaining the services that would still be operational, like ploughing, home visits for maintenance, the grocery store, the water treatment plant, and the health station for emergency medication. The crowd thinned as the meeting wound down. When it came time for questions before wrapping up, only about a dozen people remained, scattered behind Aileen, who sat stoically in the front row. Her poise appeased Evan. He noticed an easy smile on her face. *She's lived through it all*, he thought. *If she's not worried, then we shouldn't be.*

NINE

The leftover stew simmered on the stovetop. Evan stirred it with a wooden spoon as Nicole looked over his shoulder and nodded her approval.

He opened the fridge, absurdly pleased that the inside light still flashed on and absently checked the shelves. There was a big tub of margarine on the top shelf, beside a jug of nearly expired milk. Milk had become slightly cheaper with the opening of the service road and now it wasn't always condensed milk on their table.

"I should probably go to the store," he declared, staring into the fridge. "Looks like we need more carrots. And potatoes. Could use some milk too. Anything you can think of?"

"Anything in cans. Get eggs if they have some too."

"If I miss anything you can just go back tomorrow. It'll be another reason to get the kids out of the house."

The snow had let up during the meeting the day before. The roads were clear but slippery in spots. The sky remained overcast and the horizon blended with the snow in the gaps between the trees. Evan noticed snowmobile tracks in the ditches along the side of the road.

He turned right at the outdoor rink and didn't notice any activity there. *Maybe I'll check with Walter to see if he wants us to flood it for the kids*, he thought. The homes on the route leading out of the community to the service road were built much more tightly together. A high snowbank had built up at the end of the row of homes. Heavily bundled children climbed and slid down the snow on garbage bags and plastic sheets. Evan pushed down the window button to hear their chatter and laughter. It was hard to recognize the little faces concealed by toques and scarves, but he waved enthusiastically and they all waved back. He heard a distinct "uncle, uncle!" but couldn't see or make out who it was. *The kids aren't worried*, he reminded himself.

At the end of this road was the Northern Trading Post, owned by the biggest grocery chain in the country, who had a monopoly in First Nations in the North. Not only was this general store the only outlet for food, it also supplied all the hardware, household supplies, and other domestic necessities. While prices were better than they had been before the road was built, they were still outrageous compared to what people paid in the South. A two-litre carton of milk usually cost ten dollars. Sometimes it went up to fifteen.

Evan was surprised to see that the parking lot was packed. Trucks, cars, and snowmobiles were lined up sloppily in front of the store. He saw Nicole's cousin Chuck lumber out carrying a cardboard box nearly twice as wide as his frame, and he was a big man.

Evan watched Chuck put the box in the back of his truck, hop in the cab, and back out of there in a hurry. He got to the front door just as Isaiah was coming through with bulging plastic bags. He looked serious.

"Hey, shouldn't you be at work, Indian?" Evan joked, as he nudged the shoulder of his friend's red plaid lumberjack jacket.

Isaiah cracked a weak smile. "Permanent vacation, Nishnaab!" he replied. "Didn't you know?" His smile faded. "Hey, you should probably get in there. There's not much left."

"What the hell is going on?"

"I dunno, I guess people are starting to panic. My mom came by my place about an hour ago saying it was mayhem down here."

"Fuck, really? I didn't expect this."

"Me neither. I guess we didn't do a good job convincing people to relax yesterday."

"Does Terry know? What about Walter?"

"I heard Terry was down here earlier asking people to take it easy. Obviously it didn't work."

"Goddamn it."

The front door thrust open again and Sarah Whitesky blew past Isaiah and Evan.

"Whoa, whoa, whoa," Evan said. "What kind of snobby Indian are you, not even recognizing your little bro?"

She stopped suddenly. "Oh shit, sorry Ev," she said. "I didn't even see you there!" Sarah's glasses concealed much of her expression but Evan looked closely and noticed the tension around her eyes.

"So what's the rush?" he asked.

"I dunno," she replied. "I just heard everyone was buying up everything down here. I didn't wanna miss out."

"There's supposed to be another truck coming in a couple of weeks."

"Yeah, but at this point, no one knows that for sure," his sister asserted.

"Fuck sakes."

"Bro, people aren't as prepared as you," Isaiah said bluntly. Frustrated, Evan looked again at the line of vehicles hastily gathered in front of the building. A few more came down the road as people rushed out of the store holding boxes and bags.

"I gotta get going," Sarah said. "Come by later, brother. Bring the kids. Love you!" She hustled down the stairs to her idling car.

"I should go too," Isaiah said. "Don't worry because everyone else is worrying. We'll all have a good laugh about this later."

"Yeah, we better."

They nodded farewell and Evan stepped up the stairs. He pulled the white steel door open to a blast of heat. Loud chatter buzzed as people with loaded arms crowded the two checkout counters. Those who managed to secure shopping carts were only able to fill the bottom of the carts before store staff stepped in and pleaded with people to be mindful of the needs of others.

But it didn't really work. Evan stepped around people holding their finds close to their bodies. He'd joked with some of these people prior to the meeting the day before — now they avoided eye contact.

He made his way through the checkout lineups to see what was left in the aisles. The lights reflected off every surface, illuminating the empty shelves. Random green leaves, stems, and stalks lay scattered about the small produce section that hugged the close wall. Across the aisle, every bag of heavily preserved white and whole wheat bread was gone. A few boxes of soda crackers remained.

In the next aisle, a few tins of sardines were strewn across the top shelf. All the canned peas, carrots, corn — usually the least popular of the food items — were gone. On the lower shelf, a few jugs of cooking oil and some condiments like mustard were still there. Evan moved through the rest of the store, making an inventory of what else was left: dry dog food, vinegar, hot sauce, baked beans (which he grabbed), salt, baking soda. The refrigerator was barren of milk and eggs. He decided it was time to leave before he descended into panic too.

By the time he finished his walkthrough of the trading post, most of the customers had paid and left. Evan approached the counter with a can of beans in each hand. The manager, Donny Jones, eyed him up as he neared.

"Slim pickins today, eh Ev?" he joked. "What were you able to rummage up?"

"Uh . . . some beans. Came looking for milk and eggs. You're out though."

"Yep, we're out of lots of stuff."

"What the hell happened here today?"

"I dunno. People must be spooked about the power being out."

"Are you?"

"I'm just here to sell them what they need. Even if it's just a little blip, it's good for business!" Donny adjusted his glasses. "Supposed to be another truck coming in next week. No wait, it's the week after. Losing track of my days here! Either way, we'll have more stock in." He noticed Evan's blank stare. "What's wrong, bud?"

Evan shook his head. "Nothing," he replied. "Just thinking about what we got left at home. We'll be fine until the next truck comes in."

"Yeah, we'll all be fine. Guess people just get a little worried sometimes." Donny rang up the two cans. Evan paid him and left.

He stared at the road the whole drive home. He didn't notice the kids still playing on the snowbank, nor Isaiah and Tyler flooding the rink to make ice as he turned down the road that led to his house. The windows stayed shut and the stereo off while the cigarette he had lit as he left the store slowly burned out in the ashtray.

He tucked the cans under his left arm and opened the front door. The kids' movie was coming to its tender climax. They sat on the couch with their mother, eyes glued to the screen. Nicole turned to look at him when he shut the door.

Evan held up the two cans and shrugged. Nicole gave him a confused look. He said nothing and bent over to untie his boots. He hung up his coat and walked through the living room to the kitchen. He gently placed his tiny haul on the kitchen counter without saying a word.

TEN

Three more cold nights passed. The generator power would only last so long. The chief called another emergency meeting at the band office, this time just with the councillors and select staff. There was still no communication with anyone in the outside world. Terry leaned over the front desk in the main foyer, staring at his hands. The wind howled outside, blowing snow across the walkway to the front door.

"At this point," Terry started, his voice cracking. "I think we should just send out a second notice. Another meeting will just make them really panic."

Amanda Jones stepped away from the wall behind him and spoke up. "What do we tell them? We don't know anything."

The bangles on her wrists clanked as she gestured out and upward, as if to raise the confusion to the ceiling.

"I think we just tell them to be patient," said Walter, who was leaning against the desk. "We gotta tell them that this is the new status quo for the time being: to keep conserving power and water."

Evan watched each of the council members closely. They looked tired. He could see the worry and fatigue in Amanda's eyes. She was only a few years older than he was. Terry sighed. "Alright, Joanne, do up another one."

Joanne wheeled back to the keyboard. Her son Tyler moved to stand behind her. Although he was there as a rez staffer, he was also there to support his mother. She'd been having a particularly tough time over the past week. Kevin, Tyler's younger brother, was attending college down in Gibson for welding. Bright and ambitious, he planned to get his education and spend a few years working in southern Ontario before returning home. No one had been able to contact him since they had been cut off. That was over a week ago. He was one of nine from the community living elsewhere for their post-secondary education. Amanda's little brother Nick was at the same college as Kevin.

Joanne tapped out the message, printed off a copy and brought it back to the chief.

NOTICE

ONGOING COMMUNITY-WIDE POWER AND COMMUNICATIONS OUTAGE
EMERGENCY POWER GENERATION REMAINS IN EFFECT
PLEASE CONSERVE ENERGY AND WATER WHERE POSSIBLE
USE WOOD STOVES AND FURNACES AS PRIMARY HEAT SOURCES
MONITOR YOUR WATER PIPES
FOOD DELIVERY SCHEDULED FOR NEXT WEEK
PLEASE RATION IN THE MEANTIME

NEXT UPDATE MONDAY
HAVE A GOOD WEEKEND

MIIGWECH,
CHIEF AND COUNCIL

Terry turned to the others. "Should we really say there's a delivery coming?"

Walter smoothed back his greying ponytail. "Well, we originally worked it out with Donny for next week. That's still the schedule."

"Yeah, but we haven't heard from anyone in more than a week. We don't know what the fuck is going on out there!"

"Terry, relax. We'll be okay," said Walter.

"That's easy for you to say. I'm supposed to be the goddamn leader here! What am I gonna do, deliver these bullshit pieces of paper to every single fuckin' home on this rez and tell everyone it's gonna be okay? We have no goddamn answers."

"Terry, take it easy . . ." It was Amanda's turn to try to calm the chief.

"There's something seriously fucked up going on out there. Why haven't we heard from anyone? Why is the power still off? If we run out of that diesel, all the water lines are gonna freeze. Then it's gonna be fuckin' chaos here." Terry slammed his fist against the desk. "Fuck!"

Joanne jumped and the others winced or stared at their feet. Walter gazed at Terry from under his furrowed brows. Evan felt the tension rising between the two. As this crisis unfolded, he found himself gravitating towards Walter, who always kept his cool and had a calming and confident demeanour.

"Print them up, Joanne. Tyler and Evan, take them out," commanded Walter. "They're gonna want to hear something from us, and this is all we can do."

Terry inhaled deeply and looked at the floor. "I'm sorry for getting mad. You guys can all go home now. Someone will come for you when we need to meet again."

Joanne turned back to the computer screen and slid the mouse about in short bursts to print more copies. Tyler squeezed her shoulders and leaned down to kiss the top of her head. She let out a cough to stifle a sob.

ELEVEN

"Hey, wake up." Nicole nudged Evan again. He opened his eyes in the pitch-black bedroom. He couldn't tell if he was awake or still sleeping.

"Evan, wake up."

Her elbow in his side stirred him out of his deep sleep. But it was the tremble in her voice and her rigid body that really woke him.

"I'm awake. What's up?"

"I had a really weird dream."

"Oh yeah?"

"Yeah. I'm scared."

He turned to face Nicole and inched closer. "Come here,"

he said. She buried her face into his T-shirt. "What was your dream?"

"I dreamt that me and the kids were outside," she said. "And we were trying to run through the snow. But it was that kind of snow that's hard on top and real powdery underneath. Nangohns was on one side and Maiingan was on the other. I was holding their hands real tight. I was trying to run on top of the snow. But I kept falling through every couple steps. The kids would pull me back up, and we'd start running again until I fell back through. I don't know what we were running from or running to, but we had to get somewhere. You weren't around anywhere.

"The kids kept saying stuff like 'Don't worry, Mommy' and 'We're gonna make it,' but it wasn't their same voices. It was like they were elders speaking to me. They were calm. They were smiling at me every time they pulled me up from the snow. I was getting tired and they made sure I made it out of there. I was falling deeper and deeper into the snow every time the crust broke.

"Then I finally fell in over my head. I was struggling, trying to get up. The snow was getting in my eyes and in my mouth. I thought I was gonna suffocate, but they reached all the way down to pull me back up. But this time, their hands felt bigger."

Evan lay perfectly still, listening. He stroked the top of Nicole's head, soothing her while he grew increasingly frightened.

She sniffled, and he knew she was on the verge of crying. "They pulled me all the way to the surface, up to my feet. But we weren't running anymore. We were in the middle of the bush, and there was a whole bunch of other people there. There was a fire going. It looked like a winter camping site.

"I turned back to face Maiingan and Nangohns, but I saw a young man and a young woman wearing old patched snowmobile suits. They both had long hair that flowed so beautifully.

They smiled at me, and then I knew it was them. It was our kids. But they were adults. All grown up. They started talking to me in the old language, but I didn't understand them. It was a place I didn't recognize. I didn't recognize anyone else there either. I was panicking.

"Then Nangohns reached out to grab my hand. She squeezed it tight and looked into my eyes. Her eyes were so big and brown. Her cheeks were so high and proud. Her hair fell so beautifully down the sides of her face. She was the strongest and prettiest young woman. Then she reached up and touched my cheek. She said, 'Welcome home, Mommy.

"And then I woke up."

He squeezed her gently. "It's okay. It was just a dream."

He held her close to him as she fell back to sleep. He remembered his father's dream, and his eyes stayed open in the darkness as the competing omens forced the calm from his mind and body.

TWELVE

The snow came again overnight, pounding the small community at an unforgiving pace. Another thick layer of heavy snow lay on the roads, driveways, and rooftops, keeping Evan, Isaiah, and Tyler too busy to worry. They formed their usual snow-clearing formation — Evan driving the plough in the middle with the other two staggered behind him in pickup trucks outfitted with large yellow blades to clear the excess.

A full pass through the reserve took all morning and most of the afternoon. The two main roads that ran north-south and east-west and intersected right in the middle of the community were always first. Then the secondary roads that branched off from them in straight lines. The boreal region they lived in was mostly flat and allowed a practical, grid layout of the rez roads, driveways, and homes at regular intervals.

From his high seat in the plough's cab, Evan didn't notice much activity around the houses they passed, the unremitting snowfall keeping people inside. A few children played happily as full-blown winter held steady.

The convoy came to the end of the road by the Northern Trading Post, where they'd decided to stop in the parking lot for a break before driving the equipment back to the yard. The store had been closed for nearly a week, since the townspeople had ravaged its stock. *Was that really a week ago?* Evan wondered. Without any steady routine, the days were beginning to blur together and time was becoming more fluid. Despite the chaos, Evan felt more relaxed in some ways, falling into the natural rhythm of the days and the tasks that needed to be done.

They parked the trucks randomly. There was no worry of impeding any other vehicles. The air was a little milder as it usually was following a major snowfall, so they left their heavy jackets in the trucks and stood around in insulated construction overalls and sweaters adorned with the logos of sports teams and sportswear companies.

They sparked their tobacco and inhaled without saying anything. Isaiah reached into his pocket for a brown plastic bottle. He held his cigarette in his mouth while he unscrewed the black metal cap. He transferred the cigarette back to one hand and tipped the bottle back. He passed it to Evan.

Evan took the mickey of rye from Isaiah and dumped the liquor into his mouth just as quickly and effectively as his friend did. He barely tasted the burn of the cheap booze, but it warmed his throat and his innards all the way down. It was both comforting and shameful, as it always was. Tyler took it from his hand, continuing the circle.

Evan broke the silence. "Hopefully that's all the snow for a bit."

"Yeah, really. This shit ain't lettin' up," agreed Isaiah. "It's like we're getting kicked while we're down."

Tyler laughed. "As if, Izzy! What a drama queen. You guys are acting like the world is ending."

"How do you know it ain't, asshole?" Isaiah retorted.

"The end of the world is gonna be big bombs or earthquakes or some shit like that. The dinosaurs were around for like a billion years, and the only thing that could do them in was a massive fuckin' asteroid! This shit won't be slow, believe me."

"Okay, professor."

Evan shook his head and laughed. "Listen to you two geniuses." The bottle came back around and he took another swig. The faint hum of snowmobiles bounced off the woods around them.

The buzz swelled to a roar from the southeast. Tyler fixed his eyes on the service road beyond the store. It was heavily snowed in and no vehicles had driven it in weeks. But now someone was coming. Evan turned to look, and so did Isaiah, dragging off his cigarette again.

Evergreen trees concealed the bend in the road about a half-kilometre from where they stood. Trucks leaving the community always disappeared into the forest, no matter what time of year they left. And those approaching could always be heard before they were seen. Evan could hear now that there were at least two of them.

"Wonder who's coming from that way," Tyler thought aloud. "I didn't see no one head out."

Two machines pulling long sleds emerged from the trees. A bright yellow one led the way, with a black one slightly behind it and to the right. Both drivers wore dark suits and black helmets. It was impossible to tell who they were, and Evan felt his back tense. He glanced at Tyler, and then at Isaiah. Both looked uneasy.

The snowmobiles glided along the snowy surface that would become the community's winter access to the South once the surface was established. The drivers cut a path straight to Evan, Isaiah, and Tyler. They came in at full speed and slowed only as they reached the high snowbanks that dropped to the road that the team had just cleared.

The drivers eased their snowmobiles over the frozen ridge at the end of the road. The one in front raised a hand in greeting, as if he recognized familiar faces. The other did the same, and they brought their machines to a stop in front of the three Anishinaabe men and pulled off their helmets. Tyler recognized his little brother. "Holy fuck, it's Kevin!"

Kevin's short brown hair was messy, and he looked tired, but he smiled to see his brother and the road crew. The black snowmobile stopped beside him, and the second rider stood up and took off his helmet. It was Nick Jones, Kevin's best friend, looking just as dishevelled.

Tyler charged to his brother and wrapped his arms around him. "What the fuck are you guys doing here?" he shouted in excitement. Kevin buried his head in his brother's shoulder and began to sob. Evan and Isaiah rushed in and took turns hugging Nick, who was heaving with emotion and struggling to smile through a tear-streaked face. He caught his breath and said, "You guys have no fuckin' idea how good it is to see you."

"You too, bud," said Isaiah. "What's going on?"

Fear hummed in Evan's ears. *This is not good*, he thought. *Not good at all.*

"Everything's fucked up," said Kevin, as he stifled another sob. "Everything's fucked up. We had to come home."

"What do you mean, bro?" asked Isaiah.

"It's chaos down there, Izzy," replied Nick. He was referring to Gibson, about three hundred kilometres to the southwest. "The food's all gone. The power's out. There's no gas. There's been no word from Toronto or anywhere else. People are looting and getting violent. We had to get the fuck out of there."

So it's everywhere, Evan thought.

Kevin picked up where Nick left off. "We stole these sleds from school and left early this morning, when it was still dark. Shit was going bad right after the power went out. So we decided to make plans to get outta there. We stocked up on some stuff for a few days before leaving." The sleds behind the snowmobiles each held two large black hockey bags and two orange jerry cans of gas. All of the supplies were tied down tightly. "We thought we might get lost," he continued. "But getting lost and freezing to death woulda been better than just one more day in that shithole."

Evan adjusted his hat and sucked on his cigarette one last time before throwing it to the ground. It was his turn to hug and welcome the boys home. Comforting them was also an attempt to alleviate his own anxiety.

"We're glad you made it," he said. Kevin and Nick were younger than Evan and taller. They had that rangy thin build of young men who have not quite finished growing. Their almond-shaped eyes still held a youthful innocence, but they also betrayed a hardened desire to survive. "You guys should probably go home and see your parents. But don't make a big scene or nothing like that. Just try to go home quietly. Maybe park those sleds behind the store, and we'll give you rides home." Kevin and Nick nodded in agreement. So did Isaiah and Tyler. "Don't tell anyone yet about what's going on down there. We should probably talk to Terry and the council about it first. People around here are already panicking."

"Really?" asked Nick. "How bad is it?"

"The power's been out here too. And everybody bought up

everything in the store." Evan gestured with his head towards the trading post.

"Fuuuuuuck," said Kevin. He turned and ran his palm down his brown face to wipe away his tears and sweat.

"Don't worry about that, though," said Evan. "We're fine here. We got things under control. But we need everyone on the same page. So go home, let your families know you're here, and I'll go get Terry and everyone else together. Let's meet at the band office later this afternoon whenever you're ready. We'll wait for you there."

Kevin and Nick agreed and untied the hockey bags and gas cans from the carts and threw them in the back of the pickup trucks. They got back on the snowmobiles and drove them behind the store.

Kevin got in the truck with his brother, and Nick got in with Isaiah. Evan sat alone in his truck as he watched them peel out. He turned the key and waited for the initial rumble of the diesel engine to settle into a steady hum, then leaned his head on the window, staring at his friends' trucks as they dwindled into the distance.

THIRTEEN

The grey haze of the sage smoke hovered over the boardroom. The medicine continued to burn in the abalone shell on another table in the corner, pumping the healing aroma into the air. A chill remained in the room, but the temperature was steadily rising in this corner of the band office. Evan had flipped the breaker for this part of the building hours earlier and now he stood with his back against the far wall, the sleeves of his grey sweatshirt pushed up to his elbows. He watched as the others in the room milled about, reluctant to take their seats.

The long oak table was surrounded by twenty black leather chairs. The band council and senior staff held their executive meetings here, and it was always where they hosted visiting dignitaries and potential business partners — a government official coming to tour the results of a funding announcement, or a corporation looking to invest in resource extraction. But this informal gathering was unusually silent. The sun outside began to set, bouncing pink radiance off the snow and into the room.

Evan had briefed Terry and Walter. Kevin had told Tyler and their mother, Joanne, more at home. Nick had confided in his older sister Amanda, one of the councillors, and his parents. All of them were here, along with the four remaining council members and Isaiah.

Eventually, the leadership took their seats on one side of the table, while Kevin and Nick sat together on the other side with their parents. They wore nearly matching wool sweaters in slightly different shades of blue.

Terry cleared his throat. "Alright, we know why we're here." His bright red snowmobile jacket was undone to reveal a denim shirt underneath. The band councillors sat to either side of him, and Evan and Isaiah remained standing. "I just want to say we're really happy you boys made it home. We want you to know you're safe here." He looked down at the table and sighed. "It looks like it's a lot worse than we thought. I know it's gonna be hard for you to talk about this, so take your time, but we need to know what you're able to tell us. Just share what you feel comfortable sharing."

Nick and Kevin looked at each other. They were both nineteen years old, barely men. They had grown up in families that believed in teaching their kids how to live on the land and they knew how to hunt, fish, and trap. They knew the basics of winter survival. Those experiences had hardened their bodies and helped them mature, but they looked at each other now, fragile as small children. All that training could not have prepared them for what had happened.

Nick brushed his straight black hair out of his eyes. Kevin

looked to his friend and scratched the back of his head. "Okay, I'll start. I guess about a week and a half ago — I'm actually not even sure how long it was now — there was a blackout," he began. He looked down at the table, not making eye contact with anyone in the room. "I was in the welding shop at school, and it all went dark. It's in the basement of the main building and doesn't have any windows, just a big garage door that leads to a ramp outside. We waited around a bit for the lights to come back on, but then our teacher dismissed the class. So I walked across campus back to the residence, and there were a few other students waiting outside. Our keycards weren't working but security eventually let us in."

All eyes were on Kevin.

"The power came back on a couple hours later, but when I woke up in the morning, it was off again. I tried to use my cellphone but it wasn't getting any service. So I went down the hall to check on this guy." He motioned to Nick. "No one in the building really knew what was going on. We knew classes would be cancelled. We didn't go anywhere that day.

"The next day there was still no power, and no phone service. Some of the other kids in the residence started freaking out because nobody knew what was going on. The floor supervisors tried to calm everyone down, but they didn't really know what was happening either. So me and Nick left the building to see if we could find out anything."

"I think we were getting a little stir-crazy," interjected Nick. "You can't keep us Nishinaabs cooped up all day!"

Everyone laughed in a mild murmur, and Kevin continued. "The cops were at most of the big intersections, directing traffic. We asked one when the power would be back on but he didn't know. So we kept walking downtown. There were big lineups of cars and trucks at this one gas station we passed. But the pumps weren't working without the power. People were getting real mad and yelling at each other and the people working there. It was kinda ugly.

"There were also lots of cars in the parking lot of the grocery store, but it was closed. Some people were banging on the windows. The cops were there too, trying to get people to go home and wait until power came back on."

"We thought it was kinda funny," added Nick. "The blackout was only two days, but it seemed like some people were already freaking out a little bit. I was just like, 'Come to the rez, this shit happens all the time!'"

"We didn't feel like sticking around to see what would happen, so we went back to the residence," Kevin said. "When we got back there, we couldn't get in, and the security guys seemed pretty uptight about everything. When they finally let us in, we saw dozens of people sitting in the cafeteria, waiting for something. We found out it was an emergency assembly. We sat down at a table with mostly white kids. No one had been able to take showers or nothing. Everyone looked pretty bush." Kevin chuckled again. "They had sandwiches and apples and juice and that kinda stuff for us. Then someone from the college stood up and told us there was a blackout and asked us to be patient and to stay in the residence. He said the networks were down too. Some kids started getting angry, yelling that they wanted a shower or hot food. There were some security guards at the front and they sorta stepped forward to try to calm everyone down. We thought it was all pretty dumb, so we just went back to our rooms."

The more the young men opened up, the looser the others in the room became as they reconnected with them. Terry leaned back in his chair. Walter uncrossed his arms. Evan and Isaiah moved away from the wall and joined everyone else at the table. The sage had burned out but its smell lingered. It was getting dark outside.

"The next two days were more of the same," Kevin went on. "We waited in our rooms. We went down to the cafeteria for sandwiches. Every time, we pocketed an extra sandwich to save for later, just in case. We didn't want to go outside because we were worried that we wouldn't get back in. We even read books!"

"I never read so much in my life," said Nick.

"There weren't any more assemblies or updates, though," said Kevin. "Once in a while, our floor supervisor, Lance, would come by and check in on us, or tell us that someone was working on the problem. And then he stopped coming. They kept feeding us sandwiches in the caf so there was still some staff around, probably because they were hungry too. But the fruit ran out. So did the juice and milk. It was just meat on white bread. By then, it was pretty obvious that whatever was happening was really serious. So me and Nick decided to go back outside and check out what was happening.

"We had to make the security guy at the front desk promise to let us back in. But he was on edge too. He was a big white guy, looked like a football player, but his face was real pale and his eyes were bloodshot. He had a big winter coat on because it was really cold in the building by that point. It looked like he wasn't all there. I felt bad for him.

"Outside there was no one around. It looked like the campus was dead. Out on the street, the cops were gone from the intersection. There were hardly any cars out there too." Kevin paused to reach for the water bottle on the table in front of him. He twisted the cap, and the cracking of the seal was Nick's cue to pick up the story.

"It was pretty spooky," said Nick. "We heard voices from near the grocery store. We saw a whole bunch of people out front — like, hundreds. They were yelling and banging on the front door. We stopped to watch, making sure we didn't get too close.

"Then out of the blue someone threw a big rock through one of the front windows. It smashed and glass went everywhere. One guy ran up through the crowd and just heaved a garbage can right through the big window." He took a deep breath and cracked open his own water bottle, and Kevin picked the story up again. Beside him, Joanne stared at her son, her eyes fixed with worry.

"The crowd rushed into the grocery store, elbowing and shoving others out of the way. It looked like some people were getting cut on the glass because there was blood everywhere all of a sudden. Some of them were getting in fights and punching each other. We decided to get out of there.

"We ran all the way back to the residence. We decided not to tell anyone what we'd seen because we didn't want to freak them out any more than they already were. We went back to my room, and that's when we started to figure out how to get back here."

"There was a big storm later that day too," said Nick. "We knew we had to get our shit together pretty quick."

Evan looked up at the ceiling and tried to align his own memories of the recent weeks with what he was hearing. He admired their bravery and ability to make it back home. Not long ago, he'd considered them just typical teenage boys.

Kevin and Nick explained their plan to leave the mayhem in the city. Finding their way out of town and heading north was easy, they said. Both had a fairly accurate idea of the way home. And if they did get lost, they'd just try to find the hydro line and take the service road. But securing snowmobiles would be hard.

They knew where the dealerships were. Most people who owned a snowmobile on the rez had bought it from a place in Gibson. They would be locked and shuttered, maybe even abandoned by now. Floor models wouldn't do them any good anyway. They'd have to find machines that were already in use, hopefully with some gas in their tanks, since the pumps were out of service everywhere.

They'd have to siphon whatever was left in the vehicles they could find. They also needed cans to hold the gas. "The more we thought about this plan," Kevin said, "the more frustrated we got. But the people who were still left in our building were literally going crazy. Some were crying all night. Some were fighting. We had to get outta there."

They decided to pack their bags with as many clothes as possible. They put their essentials in the hockey bags and stashed the sandwiches they'd been saving deep within sweaters and jeans. The bread was growing stale but the meat was holding up because their rooms were so cold. It was the only food they'd have.

"Over the next couple of days, things got worse," said Kevin. "We were left on our own in the residence. No one from the college came by anymore. All the bottled water they left us ran out. There was no food anywhere. We sort of kept to ourselves and didn't really talk to anyone. Nobody had really talked to us much in the first place before this all happened anyway. There were fewer kids in the hallways every day. I dunno if they left town, or if something bad happened to them. But we couldn't wait around and worry.

"Security was gone. The front door's lock was broken. Anyone could come and go. I was worried there would be desperate and hungry people coming in, looking for food or shelter or anything. It was freezing. So we left our bags in our room and went to try to figure out our shit. We hid little emergency flashlights in our pockets."

Nick said they went into the campus buildings to explore. The doors were smashed open and small groups of people huddled in the corners of the foyer and in rooms off the large hallway, trying to stay warm. "They were begging us for food," his voice broke as he remembered. "Some of them looked real sick. It must have been about a week since the blackout started by that point. We couldn't help them."

"I told Nick we should go down to the shop wing. No one goes down there unless they have class. I thought we might be able to get some tools and stuff. And that's when I remembered that's where all the maintenance vehicles were kept. I thought there might even be something in the shops we could use. So we started running a bit. We looked around to make sure no one was following us. We turned down the wing, trying all the doors and they were all locked.

"We stopped in front of the door of the small-engine shop and waited a couple minutes, to make sure no one was behind us. And then I kicked it open."

"We turned on our flashlights, and I couldn't believe it," added Kevin. "It looked like no one had been in there since the power went out. Either the teacher forgot about it or just didn't care. But there were two snowmobiles in the middle of the shop. They looked pretty new, and they weren't in pieces, waiting to get fixed. I went to the hall to keep six, while Nick tried them out."

The keys were still in the ignition. Nick turned one and pulled the cord to start it. The engine revved to life. He killed it immediately, and they waited a long time before trying the other one, not wanting to attract attention. The second machine worked. Then they waited, again. Neither knew how much time they allowed to pass in the shop, but they didn't want to risk being heard or spotted, especially since they may have found their way out of the city.

Nick told them that a final scan of the shop yielded four full Jerry cans of gas in a back corner. "We didn't know if it was still any good," said Kevin, "but it was a good sign, anyways."

They left quietly through a back entrance to avoid the needy students.

"The snow was pretty deep by then," he said. "We propped the door open with a screwdriver we pocketed from the shop. We walked all the way back around to the front, tight to the side of the building, so that we wouldn't leave any footprints in the snow."

Nick squeezed his empty water bottle, crunching the plastic. When they got back to the residence building, they heard a commotion in the cafeteria as hungry students tore through the kitchen. They made for the stairs and went up to Kevin's room, where they waited out the daylight. They'd been sleeping in the same room for days by that point.

In the middle of the night they heard screams. A woman was shouting something neither of them could make out. They did their best to ignore the havoc, even as fists pounded on the door of the room where they hid. "We didn't make any noise," Kevin spoke softly. "We hoped they would think our room was empty." Even in the darkness, they were paranoid about the others seeing their packed bags or any other hints of their impending escape. They didn't sleep.

After what seemed like hours, they opened the door and cautiously carried nearly full hockey bags of clothes, food, and supplies downstairs and out the side door. They were still unsure of how they'd transport their gear with the snowmobiles, but they figured it was safer to stash their gear by the machines now, instead of scrambling for sleds or other towing implements in the heat of escape with big hockey bags on their backs.

They slipped through the frigid early morning, a half moon lighting their way. "We moved quick because of that," he added. They took the same route back and were relieved to find the door still propped open. They said they ditched their hockey bags, closed the door, and made their way back to Kevin's room. Everything was as silent as when they'd left.

"We slept for a couple hours, I guess, and then got woken up by voices outside in the hall," said Nick.

"That's when shit really started to get crazy." Kevin picked up the story again. "I opened the door and a whole bunch of people were crowded at the end of the hall. They were looking in one guy's room. His name was Dylan. I guess he got sick and died. Someone said he was diabetic. Someone else said he mighta OD'd. No one knew what happened to him.

"We walked over to look in his room. People cleared the way as we got to the door. Girls were crying. A couple of the guys were freaking out. Dylan was lying in his bed. His face was grey and his mouth and eyes were still open. It was pretty fucked up."

Nick jumped in. "All of these kids who were still in the residence weren't from Gibson. They couldn't get a hold of their parents. Their parents couldn't get a hold of them. So unless someone came and got them in those first few days, they were stuck there. They were abandoned. I think they all started to realize it when that kid died."

"This was yesterday. And that's when we really knew it was time to go," said Kevin. He talked about how they consoled the students distraught by the death, even though they weren't very close with non-Native classmates. It could have been their shyness and how they mostly stuck together. It also could have been racism. But chaos brought them together, even just for a moment. Kevin continued. "Some of them just got up and left. They didn't know where they were going, just that they had to leave too. So we just waited out the rest of the day."

But they still needed something to cart their gear, said Nick. Between them, there were four hockey bags and four gas cans. "Then I remembered the plastic sleds in storage on our floor," he said. "They were there for students to use to go tobogganing.

So we decided to take a few on the way out. We knew we'd have to double them up because they're flimsy."

"When we thought everyone was asleep, we went looking for them. Finding the storage room was hard, though, without turning on the flashlights. But we finally did. I guess those plastic sleds weren't much use to anyone, because they were still there. We grabbed them and went back to the other end of the floor to take the stairs down."

From there, they retraced their steps to the shop. The back door was as they left it, much to their relief. "So we started getting ready. We went through all the gear there and took what we thought we'd need, like a hammer, chains, a blow torch, stuff like that. We stuffed all that in the bags. I found some bungee cord, and we started tying everything to the sleds."

"We still had to get out of there," said Nick. "The shop door to the outside was locked. It was this big automatic garage door and we realized we were going to have to figure out how to raise it without power. We looked it up and down using the flashlights, and saw a chain connected to this box on the side. We were gonna have to smash that thing off the chain so we could pull it ourselves. And it was gonna be fuckin' noisy."

Kevin jumped in, his words coming faster now. "I'd seen a sledgehammer in the far corner. I went and got it and started hitting the lock thing as hard as I could."

"I started up the machines," said Nick, "because I knew as soon as he had that thing open, we'd have to hurry the fuck outta there."

"But it wasn't breaking or moving, and I dunno how many times I had to hit it. I asked Nick to take over. So he did, and it only took him a few more hits before it finally busted right off. He pulled hard on the chain to open the door. It came up real quick. And then I saw them."

Kevin took a deep breath through his nose. He held it in for a few seconds before exhaling from his mouth to ready himself to tell this part of the story. "There were two guys in big jackets and jeans and ski masks standing right there in front of us. They must have heard the banging on the door and came over from wherever they were. They asked what was going on. They sounded like white guys. I told them to fuck off and get out of the way. Then they started coming at me."

"They didn't see me though," said Nick. "So I swung the hammer at the one closest to me. I got him in the head and he went right down. The other guy was startled, so Kevin tackled him and punched him in the face a bunch of times. I told Kevin to move. He got up, and I brought the hammer down on his face."

Nick went silent and stared at the table. His mother began to weep, while his father stared sightlessly at the wall.

Kevin looked at his friend, whose face was stoic. "They were ready to kill us," he reassured him. "We got right on those snowmobiles. The sleds holding the supplies were tied tight to the back. We didn't have time to think, so we just ripped right out of there. I knew that wherever those guys came from, there were probably more like them. We went straight for the street to find our way out of town. We kept the headlamps off. It was still dark, so we didn't see anything. Luckily."

They found the road north and rode until the sun came up. Once they were safe inside the forest, they stopped to eat and refuel. They rode again until they found the hydro line, following it until they arrived at the outskirts of the rez and ran into Isaiah, Evan, and Tyler.

No one said anything at first. Nick's mom wiped her eyes. Joanne rubbed Kevin's back. Evan stood up and walked over to light the sage again. He picked up the feather that lay beside the shell and fanned the smudge gently. He approached the young men and their family, who all took their turns receiving the smudge. Afterwards, he left the shell in the middle of the table.

Terry stared at the orange embers of dried leaves and stems. The smoke thickened and rose. Still fixed on the medicine, he broke the silence. "Chi-miigwech, niniwag," he softly muttered. "Thank you to our brave young men for sharing their story. You've been through a great deal. You've survived. You made it all the way back home against incredible odds. We are thankful."

"Howah," said Walter and Jeff in agreement.

There was an eerie calm to Terry's voice, as if he hadn't yet registered the implications of what he had just heard. "Go home now and be with your families. You need to rest, and you need to eat."

"We'll figure out what to do next," Terry went on. "But for now, on behalf of council, I ask you not to tell anyone yet about what happened down there. People here are already scared — we gotta make sure we don't set them off any more. So please, try to keep a low profile for the next day if you can. We can't afford to have this whole place fall apart. We need a plan."

FOURTEEN

"Holy shit." Nicole collapsed into her chair and pressed her palms on the table. "Is this for real?"

Evan nodded.

"What are we going to do?"

He sighed. "We have to stay calm," he said. "Everyone is gonna hear all about this pretty soon. We have to make sure things don't fall apart around here."

"Well, will we be okay?"

"We have enough food, wood, gas, and other stuff to keep us going until spring. We'll be fine here at home. My parents will be fine. So will yours."

"What about Cam? What about some of the other people who aren't ready?"

"We'll have to help them to make sure they stay warm and have food to eat."

"Jesus, winter has barely even started. What about the power?"

"We'll have to talk about that tomorrow with council. There's only enough diesel to last until probably February at the latest. That's going at full power though. Luckily most people have been conserving like we asked. Some trucks were supposed to come to deliver more diesel. But we can't count on that now."

"It feels like the end of the world." Nicole stared into the darkness out the window over Evan's shoulder.

"Don't panic. We'll figure this out. Look at us here in this house — we're always ready for this kind of thing."

"It's not us I'm worried about."

Evan walked around to her side of the table and wrapped his arms around her. He bent down and kissed her cheek softly. She sniffed back tears and squeezed his arm. "We'll be alright," he whispered.

She pushed back from the table and embraced him. Her long black hair draped over his hands where he held her close. She let go and stepped back, leading him by the hand out of the kitchen. He turned off the light on the way out and followed her to the bedroom.

Their love for each other had been with them since childhood and it had been physical for nearly a decade. The only person each knew intimately was the other.

They'd hardly even been apart: Nicole had left the reserve after high school to pursue a diploma in early childhood education in the city to the south, but two months in, she was homesick, with few friends outside of kids from other First Nations, and she returned to Evan and their community for good the following spring.

Nicole took off her clothes in the darkness and heard Evan's belt unbuckle and zipper come down on the other side of the bed. She climbed into bed, eager to feel the skin of her lover against hers. They embraced under the thick covers, taking refuge in their warm pocket of sanctuary from the dangerous outside chill. They stoked the fire that began between them all those years ago.

FIFTEEN

Walter Meegis sat behind the desk in the shop's lunchroom. He leaned his chair back and propped his heavy steel-toed winter boots on the table. His jacket was wide open, and under it he wore a flannel shirt tucked into his jeans.

Chief Terry paced back and forth while Dave Meegis pored over invoices, charts, and documents about energy consumption, with Evan and Isaiah looking over his shoulders. To Evan, the numbers just bled together on the page and Isaiah looked equally bewildered. Dave was muttering to himself and neither wanted to interrupt him.

The front door blasted open and a rush of cold air followed. Evan's parents stomped in, shaking off the snow that had fallen into their hoods and coated their shoulders and sleeves. Another snowfall was blanketing the community.

"Gbakdem na?" called Dan. "You boys hungry?" He held a big steel pot, almost as wide as his torso, and Patricia carried bulging black canvas bags in each hand. Her glasses had fogged up in the sudden warmth, and she peered over them as she walked towards the small group.

Dan dropped the pot onto the table suspiciously near Walter's raised feet and chuckled. Walter pretended to scowl as he dropped his boots to the floor. "Got some stew for yas," Dan said. "Pat's got the bannock and bowls and stuff."

"Here ya go, boys," Patricia said, as she placed the bags on the table.

"Chi-miigwech, Pat," said Walter.

"No, you guys are the ones to thank. Keeping this place going."

"Well, we're doing what we can. I just wish we could tell everyone for sure when this will all be fixed."

"Ah, don't worry about it," she said with a shrug. "They can cope. Most of us didn't even have hydro or running water when we were kids!"

"Yeah, people around here sure got soft, eh?"

They both cackled, and the men around them chuckled. *If only they knew*, Evan thought.

"Okay, well we better let you boys get back to work," said Dan. "Enjoy the miijim."

"Chi-miigwech!" they all said, almost in unison as Evan's parents walked back out to their truck.

"What the fuck are we supposed to tell people, anyway?" blurted Dave.

"We'll get to that," Terry replied. "We can't let this get out of hand right now. I'm hungry!" He went to the pot, filled his bowl, grabbed a piece of bannock, and sat down.

Evan followed suit and sat down next to him. The bannock was still warm. His mouth watered and he realized he hadn't eaten since early morning. He dipped a corner of the fried dough into the thick liquid and shoved it in his mouth. The savoury sauce overpowered even the heavy salt in the bread. Before long, all of the men were eating.

Back at his table, Dave swallowed his last bite and spoke up. "Alright," he said, looking down at the sheets of paper spread out before him. "I have some good news and some bad news. What do you want first?"

"Don't fuck around, Dave. Just tell us what we need to know," ordered Terry.

Dave slid his glasses down his nose and pushed up the sleeves of his grey hoodie, revealing the faded blue tattoos on his forearms. "Fine," he said, rearranging a few of the sheets. "According to last year's energy usage, we have enough diesel to last us until the end of February, at the latest. That's what we thought all along. But if we push conservation on the people like we've been doing since we fired these back up, we may be able to stretch that until the end of March. Maybe even April. It all depends on how much wood people have. And if they get lazy.

"Since there's no guarantee we'll even get diesel again, I recommend we go ahead as we have been. We may as well ease them into spring. If people don't play along and we end up losing it all halfway through the winter, there'll be total fuckin' chaos. There'll for sure be death."

"We have to break the news to them soon," Terry muttered, resting his face in his hands. "People are antsy and they deserve to know. We'll hold another meeting. We're in a crisis and everyone's survival depends on cooperation. They're gonna panic again. It might get ugly but it has to be done. Eventually, they'll get used to it."

"When should we do it?" asked Dave.

"Tomorrow afternoon. That'll give these boys a chance to get the roads nice and clear. And this time, we definitely have to feed them."

"How do you suggest doing that?" said Evan.

"The cache. That's the only way."

Stored in a bunker below the garage at the water treatment plant was a massive cache of non-perishable food for emergency measures. A fortified secret pantry was also hidden behind one of the garage's brick walls. Thousands upon thousands of cans and boxes had been stored there for nearly two decades. Connection to the world to the south could be disrupted easily, so the chief and council of the time had passed a resolution outlining a well-maintained and updated cache of goods that could keep upwards of five hundred people fed for at least two years. Few people besides councillors knew the extent of it or where it was stored, although its existence was generally known. Gossip spread quickly in this small community, so those with specific knowledge of the food cache had kept it to themselves to protect it from raiding before it was actually needed. No one had ever really taken a prolonged disconnection from the South seriously, though.

"We'll decide what we'll need to get out of there that morning," Terry went on. "It won't be that hard to heat everything up. There'll be more people than last time."

"Alright," agreed Walter. He turned to look at Evan and Isaiah. "Evan and Izzy, you guys go get Tyler and start ploughing wherever is needed. Then it looks like we've got to send out more notices."

SIXTEEN

The angle of the sun was getting lower as the days crept closer to the winter solstice. Sunlight bounced off the pure sheen of the snow that now lay in deep piles. The wind had dropped and the air was brisk and peaceful. It nipped in nostrils and carried the smoke of furnaces and fireplaces from one end of the rez to the other. It was an idyllic winter day, even with the official beginning of the season a few weeks away, for those following the calendar. The solitude comforted Evan as he leaned against the side of the truck, smoking.

He was parked in the empty lot of the Northern. There had been no traffic here for a week. Donny Jones had shut it down shortly after the melee that emptied his shelves. There was still no contact from head office in Toronto. Some suspected Donny of hoarding food and supplies, and Evan worried that Donny's house would be targeted and that he and his family might get hurt. Along with the snow, paranoia was rising.

Evan peered past the snowy field beyond the store. The pine and spruce trees in the distance were perfectly still. He saw no wildlife. The dogs stuck to the heart of the rez, where there was more opportunity for scraps. They would be the first to go hungry if things grew more desperate. Soon the lines of their ribs would appear through their mangy coats.

If he had more time, and his snowshoes with him, he would have traipsed through that snowy field to look for tracks. But he was on the clock, waiting for Tyler and Isaiah to finish up their last rounds and meet here before delivering notices throughout the First Nation.

Evan pinched off the end of his smoke and stepped on the remnants. He was beginning to run low. If there was no way to get to the closest town or city, there was no way to get man-ufactured smokes. Filtered cigarettes would become a luxury. He snorted — this was one way to finally quit. As he opened the door and stepped up on the metal runner to get back into the warm cab, he heard the buzz of a snowmobile. It star-tled him, so he stepped back down to the ground. He tried to remember if it was the first he'd heard since Kevin and Nick had arrived home.

He looked across the field and then back toward the heart of the rez. Nothing. Yet the sound built, coming from the service road. He felt butterflies in his gut.

A snowmobile emerged through the trees, kicking snow high into the air. This machine was bigger than the ones Kevin and Nick had rolled in on. And even from this distance, the driver appeared tall and burly. Whoever it was blazed through the snow, easily controlling the machine and the heavy trailer attached to it.

Who the hell could that be? It didn't look like a machine from the rez. Kevin and Nick hadn't said if they'd mentioned their escape to anyone in Gibson. *Was it someone who came from down there? Why would they come all the way here?*

The hum intensified, and Evan remembered that he was still alone. He looked back up the road and didn't see his friends' trucks. He was going to be the sole contact at the de facto gate to the rez.

Evan stepped back up into the cab, reached for the rifle behind the bench, and switched off the safety. He realized he was likely in the driver's sight now, so he stepped back to the ground and looped his arm through the red strap to rest the loaded gun behind his shoulder. He didn't want to have to use it.

He rolled his head around his neck to ease the tension in his shoulders. He looked back up the road. Still, no trucks. He squeezed and released his fists rapidly in his thin thermal gloves.

With all the recent snowfall, the snowbank at the end of the plough zone was almost as high as a pickup truck. The snowmobile sped towards it without slowing. Evan felt the driver's eyes on him through the helmet's visor. His square frame marked him as a man. *He's coming right for me*, thought Evan.

The engine finally slowed as it approached the dip down to the road. The driver guided the skis down the embankment and hit the gas slightly to catch the track on the icy road. The sled behind fell to the ground with a thud. It was almost as big as the snow machine itself.

The entire rig inched forward. Everything was black — the snowmobile, the sled, the boots, the suit, and the helmet. It stopped a comfortable distance from where Evan stood. *Close enough to be a target.* He kept his hands in front of him, mindful of the rifle that lay over his shoulder.

The driver slowly raised both hands, as if to indicate he meant no violence or confrontation. The gesture caught Evan off guard, but he nodded and raised his own hands. The driver lowered his hands and killed the engine. It sputtered into silence as the driver stood, putting his hands up once again to ensure he displayed no sudden, threatening movements.

Trees cracked under the weight of snow in the still, crisp air. As he stood up, the stranger's stature stunned Evan. He was a beast of a man who was invading his people's space.

"I come in peace." The man's voice was a guttural baritone, and the words echoed across the barren landscape. Then he started to laugh, a mild chuckle, that quickly escalated into sharp guffaws.

Evan didn't know whether to aim his rifle, extend his hand, or laugh with him. The man was well over a head taller than he was. The heavy snowmobiling jacket accentuated his bulk. He didn't look armed, but Evan was certain he had guns. He decided he better say something.

"As the old saying goes," Evan began sternly, "come in peace or leave in pieces."

The man stopped laughing and stood silent. Then he erupted in boisterous laughter. "That's a classic, brother!" he shouted as he leaned over, grabbing at his gut. But it sounded insincere and did nothing to ease Evan's anxiety.

"Who are you?" Evan asked.

The large figure caught his breath and stood upright again. "The name's Scott. Justin Scott."

"What are you doing here?"

"Well, I was in the neighbourhood, so I just figured I'd stop by." The helmet muffled his voice, and Evan couldn't get a read on him without seeing his face. "Oh, how rude of me!" Scott added. He unclipped the strap on his chin and lifted his helmet off his head, revealing a wide, bald dome. His eyes squinted in the bright daylight, but everything else about his facial features was large. His bulbous nose complemented his wide mouth, contained by a square jaw. The wide, unzipped collar of his thick jacket and the black turtleneck sweater he wore under- neath obscured his neck, but it looked as wide as his massive head. He made no motion to approach Evan.

"What are you doing here?" Evan repeated.

"Well, friend," Scott continued. "As you may well know, the proverbial shit has hit the fan. I'm just looking for a nice, friendly place to lay my head for a little while."

"Why here?"

"Far away from so-called civilization seems like the best place to be right now."

"How did you find us?"

"Easy. I just followed the other sled tracks."

The hair rose at the back of Evan's neck. *Goddamn it*, he thought. *He followed Kevin and Nick.*

Evan heard one of the trucks approaching behind him. *Finally*. It was Isaiah in his big red diesel pickup. Isaiah took in the standoff and the rifle as he pulled his truck next to Evan's. He jumped out, leaving his truck running, and stepped to Evan's side.

"What's going on?" he asked.

The sun glanced off Scott's bald head. "We're getting acquainted."

"Who are you?"

"My apologies. The name's Justin Scott."

Isaiah turned to Evan, who was monitoring the visitor. Wary of Scott's every move, Evan didn't even acknowledge Isaiah.

"What do you want?" Isaiah prodded.

"Well, as I was just explaining to your friend here — sorry,

I didn't catch your name?" Scott said to Evan, stepping off the snowmobile.

"It's Evan."

Scott looked to Isaiah. "And what's your name?"

There was an awkward silence. Evan's heart pounded in his eardrums. He didn't want the situation to escalate. He shot Isaiah a glance to prompt him to respond to the stranger.

"Isaiah," he finally replied.

"Evan and Isaiah," Scott repeated, taking a few long strides towards them. "Nice to meet you." He walked closer and took his thick gloves off, extending his bare, calloused white hand in greeting.

He turned to Evan first, who reluctantly obliged. His rough, meaty palm dwarfed Evan's. The handshake was half goodwill, half intimidation. Scott let go and shook Isaiah's hand the same way. Evan noticed that the top of Isaiah's head came up only to Scott's hard blue eyes, and Isaiah was a tall man.

"Where were we? Oh, yes, that's right. I was just explaining why I'm here. Well, my Ojibwe friends, I'm here for the same reason everyone else is: to breathe the fresh northern air. I also want to taste the finest moose meat — I hear they're bountiful up here. And I hear the hospitality of the Ojibwe is unrivalled."

Isaiah narrowed his eyes. "Are you fucking with us?"

"Now, son, no need for vulgarities. I told Evan, I come in peace."

"I'm not your son."

"Izzy, just chill out," Evan scolded him.

Scott's smile faded. He cracked his jaw, shifting it from side to side. "I have a good feeling that you boys know what's happening. I don't think you woulda grabbed your rifle, Evan, if you weren't on edge," he said. He shifted his focus to Isaiah. "Now Isaiah — may I call you Izzy?"

"No."

"Isaiah, I was just starting to tell Evan about how I followed two weaving sled tracks out of the city and up here."

"Fuck," Isaiah muttered under his breath.

"I'm sure whoever made those tracks told you about the situation. Quite honestly, it's bad. Down south is the last place you want to be right now."

"Is that why you're here?"

"I'm a man of the land, fellas. Right now, I'm getting the lay of it."

"Cut the bullshit, man," Evan commanded.

"I apologize, Evan. The trail has taken a bit of a toll. I've had a lot on my mind, and a lot of time to think about it." The frigid air didn't seem to bother his bare head. "What's the situation here?"

"I don't think you've earned the right to ask questions here yet," Evan replied.

"Well, I'll tell you my side of things, then," said Scott. "Ten days ago, we lost everything at once, power, satellite, comms. It went to shit pretty quick. What do people here know?"

"Everything is out here too," Evan said grudgingly. "We don't know much. We know about Gibson because two of our boys came back yesterday. The boys you followed."

"I hate to break it to you, boys," Scott said, "things are gonna get worse. How much food is here?"

"Enough. We're a community of hunters." As soon as the words left his mouth, he knew he was exaggerating.

"Good. I'm a bit of an outdoorsman myself. I think I'll fit in well here."

Scott's smile did nothing to reassure Evan. He was on the run, that was clear. He needed a place to hide. *What else does he know?* wondered Evan. *Why does he want to be here?* He studied the rig behind him and noticed large hard cases tied down to the steel sled. "What's in the back there?"

Scott turned to glance at his ride. "Oh, just winter supplies," he said. "Everything I need for winter survival. I've been prepared for this for a long time."

"Yeah, looks like it." Evan glanced over the cases another time, imagining what was inside. He assumed a small arsenal.

"So you're planning on staying a while, I guess, eh?" said Isaiah.

"If I'm welcome, and for however long you'll have me."

"That's not up to us. We're gonna have to talk to chief and council."

"May I meet them?"

"It'll take some time. We're waiting for someone else to meet us here. We'll send him to get someone when he gets here."

"Fair enough."

White strangers weren't a rarity — non-Anishinaabeg came regularly. Some were government officials, others had business interests, and there were usually a few church and health people on assignment to the rez. White labourers also came up to fill employment gaps the community itself couldn't meet. A few stayed for good, after finding love and starting families. But their community was remote. No one just "stopped in."

Evan pulled his pack of smokes out of his pocket and tipped it in Scott's direction, raising his eyebrows. Scott shook his head slightly. Isaiah paced until the last plough rolled down the road to lift the uncomfortable standoff. Isaiah waved Tyler in.

Tyler pulled the large black truck up to Evan and Isaiah. He opened his window and mouthed "what the fuck?" as Isaiah stepped up to his truck.

"He says his name's Justin Scott," Isaiah whispered over the rumble of the diesel engine. "He just showed up on that snowmobile. It sounds like he's from the city. He followed Kevin's and Nick's tracks up here."

"What does he want?"

"He wants to stay here. He hasn't really said much yet. He's really weird. I don't trust him."

"Well, what are we gonna do?"

"Go get Terry and whoever else you can find. Walter. Get Walter too. They're gonna have to decide. I don't think we got any choice, though. He seems dead-set on staying here."

"Goddamn it. People are gonna shit themselves if they see him."

"Yeah, I know. So go get council as soon as you can and bring them back."

"Alright, I'll be right back. Take these first." Tyler handed Isaiah another stack of paper before he put the plough into reverse to drive back up the road.

"He didn't want to join the party?" asked Scott.

"He's going to get the chief and some councillors."

"Well, I hope they get here soon. We're not much use to anyone just standing out here in the cold. I'm sure you boys still have a job to do."

Without answering, Isaiah split the stack of flyers Tyler had given him and handed Evan half. He looked down at the paper.

COMMUNITY MEETING

TOMORROW AT NOON IN THE GYM
UPDATE ON POWER OUTAGE
PLEASE CARPOOL IF POSSIBLE
LUNCH WILL BE PROVIDED
REMEMBER TO TURN OFF ALL LIGHTS WHEN LEAVING HOME

MIIGWECH,
CHIEF AND COUNCIL

"What's that you got there, boys?" Scott asked.

"Nothing, just an update we gotta deliver," replied Isaiah.

"What are you telling them?"

"Don't worry about it."

They stood in awkward silence, awaiting the return of Tyler's pickup. Evan kept his eyes fixed on Scott, but grew increasingly uncomfortable as the seconds dragged on. Isaiah nervously shuffled his feet and darted his gaze from his friend, to the stranger, to the ground, and back again. Scott eased his stare between them with a smirk on his face. When the truck arrived, Terry and Walter were squeezed into the cab with Tyler. He stopped in the middle of the road, and the two older men got out while Tyler remained behind the steering wheel with the engine running.

Terry looked at his two young staffers, trying to find clues in their expressions. Then he turned to the strange man before them. Walter walked calmly behind him. "So what do we have here?" Terry asked.

Scott turned his attention to Terry and Walter as they approached. He took a few easy steps in their direction, hand outstretched.

"Good afternoon, my name is Justin Scott, and I'm from Gibson." He directed his greeting at Terry first, as if sensing he was the more important of the two. The arrogance that had been in his voice when he'd been talking to Isaiah and Evan gave way to respect, though Evan questioned its sincerity.

"I'm Terry Meegis, and I'm the chief here." Terry shook Scott's hand and waved in Walter's direction. "This is Walter Meegis. He's one of our councillors."

"It's an honour to meet you, Chief, and Councillor Meegis," Scott replied as he shook Walter's hand. Scott put his hands on his hips, while Walter put his own in the pockets of his jacket.

"So what can we do for you, Mr. Scott?" asked Terry.

"Well, sir, I humbly come before you asking for refuge in your community. I'm sure you're aware of the situation in the city. It's getting worse, and I feared for my safety. So I escaped in the darkness early this morning."

Evan watched Walter eye the large man. He guessed Walter was coming to the same conclusion he did after scrutinizing Scott's figure — that he was somewhere in his late thirties or early forties. Clearly able-bodied.

"I followed two lines of snowmobile tracks to the power lines, which led me all the way here. I understand two of your young ones made their way back here, escaping the city like I did. I didn't know where the trail would lead me. But here I am. And now, I'm begging you to allow me to stay here for the time being. I saw some pretty horrific things in the last few days."

His voice cracked and he looked down at the hard-packed icy snow at his feet. The sudden vulnerability shocked Evan. He didn't seem like the same cocky person who had prodded them moments earlier. Evan wasn't sure what to make of this about-face, but it didn't make him trust Scott any more. He didn't believe everything about this stranger's story, either.

"I'm sorry to hear of your hardships," Terry responded. "We're just starting to understand what's going on here. It sounds pretty messed up. But why should we take you in?"

Scott stood straighter. "Well, Chief Meegis, I'm a hunter, much like you are, I assume. I can help provide for your community. I'm a survivalist. I know how to live on this land without the comforts and luxuries people in the South have become too dependent on. I know all about emergency management. I can help your people adapt to this situation."

"Why should we trust you?" Terry asked.

"Because what you see is what you get," he said. "I come to you with only the intention of survival and the hope of being part of a community. We're only going to get through this with each other."

"What's in the boxes?"

"Supplies. Hunting gear. Food. Clothes. A tent. The essentials."

"How do we know you're alone, like you say?"

"You just have to believe me."

"How can we be sure no one followed you?"

Scott shrugged. "I guess you can't. But as your boys probably told you, no one down there was ready for this. They're lucky they made it out."

Terry pursed his lips. "Well, as I'm sure you can appreciate, Mr. Scott, we're gonna have to discuss this. Please excuse us." He turned his back on Scott and motioned for the others to follow him behind the biggest plough. "Take your time," Scott said, flashing a toothy smile as they disappeared. Tyler remained in the truck, watching the newcomer.

They huddled behind the plough. Terry scratched his beard, and Walter tugged again at his ponytail.

"So what are we gonna do with him?" Walter asked.

"We can't just send him back," answered Terry.

Walter gritted his teeth. "The fuck we can't!"

"What's gonna happen to him if he goes back down there? Or if he has to find somewhere else to go?"

"Who the fuck cares! I don't trust him."

Evan piped up. "I don't trust him either, Terry." It was unusual for him to speak out, especially in a circle with his elders.

Terry sighed. "We may be able to use him, though," he protested. "He could pull more weight than a lot of the deadbeats in this goddamn rez."

Evan thought of his brother Cam and his friends who passed their days playing video games and smoking dope. Evan realized he hadn't visited Cam lately and decided he would go over and check on him later.

"We can't just turn him away," Terry continued. "It's not our way. We can't just send him off to die."

"Alright, we let him stay," Walter conceded. "But he has to contribute. He has to hunt. He has to gather wood. Where are we gonna put him, though?"

"We can put him in the health station," Terry suggested. The community nurses rotated in two weeks at a time and the crisis had hit the week before another one was to come in from Gibson. The health station was empty. This wasn't the first time the rez had been left without a nurse, and when it happened, the few with first-aid training — like Nicole or Walter — stepped up for basic care.

"There are beds in there," Terry went on. "There's a kitchen. That means we'll have to put the heat on in there, though. But eventually we'll put him in someone's house. As soon as he proves he can be a part of this community and that he can be trusted."

"So what then," Evan asked. "Do we make him get one moose a week or what?" He was only half-joking.

Walter chuckled. "That's actually not a bad idea."

"No, it's not," Terry said. "But we'll worry about that later. For now, let's just tell him the deal."

"What about the rest of council? Shouldn't we talk to them first?" asked Walter.

"I don't think we have time. People are gonna eventually see us down here with him and they'll come see what's going on. We should get him out of the way."

"Okay, make him promise to keep a low profile until after the meeting. People are gonna shit themselves if they see this big fuckin' white guy out and about."

Scott accepted their offer, saying he was humbled and

honoured to join them. The late afternoon sun stretched their shadows as they got into the trucks to convoy to the community complex. Walter got behind the wheel of Isaiah's truck with Terry in the cab and Justin Scott lying flat in the back. Isaiah drove Scott's snowmobile. They rolled out of the parking lot, veiled by the encroaching twilight.

SEVENTEEN

The sage smoke billowed high and dissipated. As it smouldered into ash, the scent weakened, giving way to the strong smell of woodsmoke now woven into the jackets and sweaters of the men and women in the crowd.

Nearly every seat was taken. There were more than twice the people gathered than the last time, and there was a more subdued hum about the room. There were fewer children in the crowd. People had quiet, serious conversations with their neighbours. And those who were silent gazed straight ahead, lips pinched with worry.

The chief had met with the council the evening before, just after Justin Scott's appearance at the edge of town, to settle on a course of action. A stranger's arrival didn't sit well with any of them.

"Gchi-manidoo miigwech." Aileen finished the prayer, but Terry stayed sitting, tapping his fingers on the table in a nervous staccato. The first two fingers on his right hand were stained a foul yellow from nicotine. He'd been chain-smoking since the power went out. He shared the general worry that cigarettes would soon run out too, but he couldn't seem to cut down. He stood up and pulled at his thick blue sweater. "Good morning. Thank you all for being here. We asked you to come so we could bring you up to speed on what's happening. We still don't know what caused the problem or when the power will be back on. So we're gonna ask you to keep being careful with how you use it. Jeff here will tell you more later in the meeting.

"We have some new information that gives us a better idea of what's happening everywhere else. Some of you have probably heard by now about Kevin Birch and Nick Jones, who returned home from the city two days ago on snowmobiles."

The room buzzed with the news. Terry let the murmurs subside before continuing.

"We've had a meeting with the boys, and they've told us that there's a blackout down there too. It happened around the same time our power went out. So it sounds widespread. They decided to come home because the city people weren't prepared and things were getting worse pretty quick. But they're home and they're safe. Right now, they're just asking to be with their families, so please leave them be. You can come to us with your questions."

From his spot behind the table, Evan scanned the room. He saw his mom, dad, and sister, Sarah, sitting to the side about halfway back. They had all kept their dark snowmobile jackets on. Most people did now. A persistent chill pervaded every room on the rez. Once again, his brother didn't seem to be there.

"It looks like there's enough fuel to keep the power on throughout the winter," said Terry. "But only if everyone co-operates. As long as there's power for the water treatment plant, it can keep pumping in water from the lake. Our goal is to keep running water in your homes for the whole winter. If we run out of diesel for the generators, we'll have no water in our homes. It's that simple.

"Our biggest concern right away, though, is food." As Terry steeled himself to explain the upcoming rationing, Evan scanned the crowd for Donny Jones, the Northern's manager. He couldn't see him anywhere. *That asshole really should have handled things better*, Evan thought. *And he should have the balls to be here.*

"We don't think we'll be getting a truck anytime soon," Terry began. "The service road is snowed in, and we don't know if Hydro is going to be around to make it drivable for the winter. It might be too late, with all the snow that's already come." Fear squeezed itself into the gym.

"We all know there wasn't enough food at the trading post to last us for the rest of the winter. And all that food is gone now anyway. So we have to use our emergency supply. There is a cache that will last us for a while. But again, we have to be smart about it. We're going to assess each home's need, and set rations according to that. That means we'll be visiting your homes over the next few days to see what you have. I know it's not ideal, but it's the only way we can do this fairly."

There was an eerie silence among even the most outspoken of the rez people, the corn soup and bannock they'd eaten before the meeting still settling in their bellies.

Someone in the back shouted, "So I spend all summer fishing and all fall hunting to feed my family in the winter, and the lazy-ass people in this rez get food for free?" Evan tried to spot the heckler. He was there with Isaiah to serve as security in case the assembly got out of hand.

"Yeah, what the hell?" someone else called out.

Walter rose to his feet and attempted to restore order. "Okay, okay, calm down," he shouted into the racket. "Quiet!" His booming baritone hushed the entire gym.

"Nobody's getting any kind of special treatment. And we're not gonna keep any food or supplies from anyone. This is a goddamn crisis! We have to act like a community. We're going to support each other until this all gets sorted out."

Evan wondered whether this meeting had served any good purpose.

Walter took a deep breath, lowered his wide chin to the white buttons of his denim shirt, and buried his face in his rough hands. He dragged them slowly down his cheeks, pulling his lower eyelids down and exposing his bloodshot eyes as he exhaled. "I'm sorry," he said. "This has been a tough time for everyone here. I'm sorry I yelled."

"It's okay, Walter," shouted someone from the back.

"Yeah, Walter, it's okay," said a new voice through the open door at the back. Everyone turned to see the tall, bald, muscular white man walk into the room. His heavy workboots made loud thuds on the tiled floor. Justin Scott had arrived for the whole crowd to see.

"What the fuck is he doing here?" Terry whispered to Walter, loud enough for Evan to hear.

"We told him to stay put!" Walter growled. He shot a cutting gaze at Evan, as if expecting him to contain the situation. Evan could only shrug.

The crowd's uneasy buzz grew. Evan caught his father's eye, who furrowed his brow and mouthed "Who's that?" as Patricia bit her thumbnail beside him. Evan tried his best to keep his face blank. Scott stopped and finished his sentence. "We'll get through this. Together." He beamed and raised his fists high above his head and pumped them.

Evan's cousin Mark Whitesky shot to his feet and yelled, "Who the fuck are you?" as Evan and Isaiah moved to stave off any confrontation.

Walter tried to placate the room. "Calm down, everyone. Please allow me to introduce Justin Scott. He's arrived from the South and is with us for a little while."

"Aaniin, everybody," Scott said, as if he thought he could pacify the crowd with a greeting in their language. He folded his big arms over his chest, smirked, and nodded, his body-builder's neck even wider than his large head.

"We were going to wait to introduce Mr. Scott," Walter said, staring sharply in Scott's direction. "I guess we just got our lines crossed." He let the last part of his statement float in the air.

"Oh, my apologies," Scott said. "I didn't mean to interrupt. I just wanted to say hi and meet some of the fine people here. I'm here to help. I'm sure we'll all get to know each other very well over the next little while."

"Miigwech, Mr. Scott," said Walter before Scott could say anything else. He looked over his shoulder and said loudly, "Evan, maybe it's time you showed our guest around." The councillor cocked his head in Scott's direction and diverted people's attention back to the front of the gym, saying, "Okay, now Debbie McCloud is going to explain how the food distribution is going to work," he said, welcoming the small woman outfitted in a pink tracksuit. She pushed her glasses up her nose and stood, explaining the plan in a booming, cheerful voice.

"Hey bud!" chirped Scott as Evan approached. The breezy greeting made Evan's skin crawl. He nodded for Scott to follow him.

Once they'd rounded the corner into the hallway that connected the gym and the health station, Evan turned to face him.

"What the fuck are you doing, man?" he whispered harshly. "We asked you to stay put."

"I must not have heard properly," Scott replied. "I thought I was to meet you all in the gym after the meeting. I thought it would have been done by now."

"You could have waited when you saw it was still happening."

"But if I'm gonna be a part of this community, shouldn't I know what's happening?"

"You're not a part of this community."

"Oh no?"

"No. You have to step up, just like everyone else. And then we decide if you can stay."

"You don't think I can?"

"I don't know you."

Scott towered over Evan under the pale glow of the fluorescent lights above them. Evan knew that he was no match for this man in a fight. He wasn't intimidated; though he wasn't quite sure why. He eased back from their confrontation and the stranger relaxed.

"Well, let's get to know each other then. So what of this tour?"

Evan decided to show him the shop and then take him to the band's main offices. For the first time, Evan considered the man's own vulnerability. *He's stranded,* thought Evan. *He needs us more than we need him.*

EIGHTEEN

Maiingan stood on the counter on his tiptoes and peered into the dark cupboard. He gripped the bottom shelf with his left hand, a little nervous about the height from the floor.

"Okay, sweetie, tell me how many big cans there are," asked Nicole.

The boy reached in with his right hand extended and touched each one as he counted the cans of tomatoes. "One . . . two . . . three . . ." He carefully tallied the wide tins wrapped in the familiar no-name label. "Four . . . five . . . six . . . seven!" His voice piped with pride when he got to seven.

"Good! Way to go, bud," said his mother. "Now do it one more time just to make sure." A tedious task for any older child, this was a fun counting exercise for Maiingan. He was thrilled to be able to help his mother with an important chore. And to be able to stand on the counter.

"Alright, my boy, now do the little yellow ones," said Nicole. He opened the right cupboard and inspected the rows of cans of corn. "Found them!" he proclaimed. He proceeded to count and declared that there were nine in there.

Nicole jotted down *9* next to *whole corn* in an elementary-school scribbler. When they finished in the kitchen and in the hall pantry, she planned to tally the contents of the bigger pantry in the basement. But she would wait until Evan arrived home to watch the kids so she could do it on her own. She wanted to keep the lights off in the basement for now and knew she'd be faster without her son later.

She planned on counting the upstairs stores once again anyway. Not that she didn't trust her son's skills. She just needed something else to do to pass the time.

Nicole had grown up in a house much like the one she shared with Evan and her children. She had two older sisters. Geraldine, the eldest, lived on the other side of the rez with her husband and three boys, and Danielle had moved to Toronto for school when she was nineteen and had been there ever since. Her husband, Sean, was not Native and was often teased by everyone in their wider family, but he was loved deeply nonetheless.

Nicole thought now of her seven-year-old nephew, Will, and what might have become of him since the rez had been cut off from the world. She pictured his toothless grin and bright blue eyes. She wondered if Toronto was blacked out too. She thought of the chaos she'd heard about in Gibson and pictured her young nephew frightened as hungry mobs rolled through the bigger city streets where he lived. Fear crept up her back and she shuddered. She shook the thought from her head and focused again on Maiingan.

"Okay, bud, how many little green ones? Those are the peas," she said.

"Ewww, peas? I don't want to count them!" Maiingan scrunched up his little face. "Peas are gross!"

Nicole snickered. "You don't have to eat them. Just count them!"

"Okay," the boy reluctantly agreed. "One . . . two . . . three . . ."

"One! Two! Three!" Nangohns echoed from the table. She raised her head from her colouring book, apparently in need of attention. Nicole's heart warmed every time she heard her daughter's voice. "Can you count too, baby girl?" she asked. The three-year-old nodded enthusiastically and looked back down to the erratic lines of blue and orange crayon that breached the outlines of the picture she was colouring in.

Nicole heard feet stomping up the stairs to the front door and turned to see Evan's head loom into the window frame, his breath visible as he exhaled. He opened the door, and Maiingan shouted, "Daddy! I've been helping Mommy count the cans!"

"Daddy!" Nangohns echoed. Nicole helped the boy down from the counter as the girl leaped off her chair.

"Aaniin, binoojiinyag!" he boomed. They ran up and wrapped their arms around him, cold coat and all. He leaned down to kiss the tops of their heads while he tried to wiggle out of his coat with the children stuck to his legs.

"Hey," Nicole said as he walked over to kiss her. They hugged, holding on tightly. "Ah, this feels solid. This feels safe," she said into his shoulder.

"Huh?" he said.

"Oh, nothing. Just glad you're home."

It was unclear to them both if this was the shape of their lives now. Evan still held out hope that it was temporary, but Nicole was less certain.

Evan's workload had increased substantially with the electricity rationing. He kicked off his boots and collapsed on the couch. It was well past noon and he had been up since before dawn, ploughing the roads and then driving Candace North around to continue inventorying people's household food stores. It was their third day — an intense, tiring routine that involved taking a lot of questions and requests from the worried townspeople. "When's this blackout gonna be over?" most asked. "We don't have no more meat!" declared others. "You sure this food is gonna last?"

He was thankful that he didn't have to answer the questions. He just had to go through refrigerators, cupboards, pantries, and deep freezers to register what people had so the council could determine what would be needed in the rollout of rations. He was disappointed to discover how few hunted anymore. Many had grown complacent in the rut of welfare.

As he lay on the couch, Evan thought about the remaining homes they had to get to. Images of pickup trucks, blowing snow, and counting cans and weighing moose meat whirled through his mind.

He was driving the plough through a thick layer of heavy snow on the road by the rink. The truck struggled as the road became tougher to navigate the closer he came to the heart of the community. The overcast daylight cast everything in a sickly grey glow.

He drove up to the main intersection. He looked to his right to see if anyone was at the rink, but he could see that the metal roof had caved in. Ahead of him, the snow was nearly as high as the truck's headlights. The wheels spun but gradually caught some traction and he kept ploughing his way to the community complex with the band office, school, and health station.

No one was around. It looked like no other vehicles had passed these roads in a very long time. The ghostly silence unnerved him. He reached the driveway to the community complex and frantically pulled on the steering wheel to make the turn, but the truck got stuck at the bottom of the hill.

Desperate, he tried to open the door, but the deep snow blocked his exit. He bodychecked the door with his shoulder, but it barely budged. He shifted in his seat to face the door and raised his feet to try to kick it open with both legs. That didn't work either. So he kicked at the window to smash it open. His feet passed through, and glass flew into the cab and out onto the snow, now as high as the window itself. Still, no snow fell from the sky above.

Evan climbed out headfirst, shards of glass tearing at his jacket and pants. He tried to stand on the snow, but fell up to his thigh with each step. He lay on his belly to crawl the rest of the way to the band office. With each pull, the thick snow crushed into his face. It went into his nose and mouth, and he struggled to breathe. He had to pause to come up for air. He looked behind him, and saw a trail of blood all the way to the truck, where only the blue roof was now visible. The air remained dry and still but the snow grew denser and seemed to rise from beneath him.

Suddenly, the top began to freeze, taking hold of his arms, legs, and torso. It thickened with each lunge forward. He kicked to free his legs and feet as ice scabbed over the snow. He was sinking into the lighter stuff below and he struggled to hold himself up on the crust, kicking and heaving himself forward with as much force as he could rally. He rolled over onto the ice, exhausted, and lay on his back for a moment to catch his breath before struggling to his feet. The crust was now thick enough to support his weight, so he ran towards the building in the distance. He looked behind to find the gaping hole he'd escaped from, but it had already disappeared. A trail of blood still followed him. He didn't know where he was cut.

He fixed his eyes on the front door of the complex. It appeared to sink as the snow got higher. He was running out of time. He needed to get in at all costs. He gasped for air as he pumped his legs as hard as he could. The creeping snow was now nearly as high as the door handle. Just steps away, he jumped forth with his shoulder down and his head tucked into his chest. His body hurtled through the glass. He got up and pulled open the second set of doors and went through, locking them behind him. The snow piled through the broken glass and filled the space between the doors.

It grew dark as snow swallowed the building. A fire burned at the far end of the foyer, flicking orange light onto the walls and ceiling. He looked up to see a frozen crust grow over the skylight, blocking out the overcast sky.

The fire in the back made no smoke or heat, only light. He walked cautiously towards it. The whole space was barren. No furniture, no supplies, no signs of any kind of human presence. As he approached the fire, he noticed strange, dark stacks lined up against the walls. They looked like rolls of blankets. But the closer he came, he realized they were bodies, frozen stiff, wrapped in blankets, and piled three-to-four high against the Gyprock walls.

He stopped and struggled to breathe. His heart pounded but his feet felt frozen. He stumbled forth, almost drunkenly. The fire danced above the floor, suspended ominously.

His heavy feet trudged slowly towards the pile of bodies on the left. Wrapped in fading material and stacked together, they all looked the same size. These were all adults, he concluded. *Thank god there are no children here.* The room seemed to stretch longer the closer he got to the wall. The row of frozen bodies extended much farther than he had originally realized.

He looked back down and saw thick black hair sticking out the end of a grey wool blanket. He saw his hand rise to reach for it. His fingers stroked cold, coarse hair. He ran his palm across the stiff, frigid scalp and he pulled the blanket away from the face.

The dream shocked him awake before he saw who it was. He yelped as he jolted up.

Nicole came around from the kitchen and looked at him with concern on her face. "You alright?"

Evan propped himself onto his left elbow and rubbed his eyes. "Yeah," he croaked in a hoarse voice. "Just a messed-up dream."

NINETEEN

Scott exhaled and relaxed his shoulder as the bull settled in his scope. He squeezed the trigger and the loud crack scattered the other nearby moose. His target fell to the snow. "Fuckin' got 'im! Woohoo!" he belted out.

Dan, Isaiah, Evan, and Jeff Whitesky crouched in the snow behind the newcomer. "Looks like you weren't kidding, zhaag-naash," said Jeff, pushing his glasses up his nose. "You can shoot."

"Ha ha!" Scott gloated. He twisted his torso to face the men behind him and squinted into the cold white landscape. "It's been a long time since I bagged a moose in the winter. They're basically like sitting ducks out there, eh?"

The rest rose to their feet behind him, now that the 'other moose had disappeared into the sparse bush. "Yeah, after the rut, the bulls tend to stick together in the winter," Dan explained. "They don't move too much either."

"But we don't like to do this much, hunting them in the winter," added Jeff. "It's kinda like cheating. It's not the Anishinaabe way to take more than you need. Back in the day, before beef roasts were shipped in here, we only did it when we needed to. Only during the desperate times."

Scott put the safety back on his .30-30 rifle and threaded his big arm through the shoulder strap. "Well, I'd say these are desperate times," he said. "That's why we're out here, isn't it?"

"No, we're out here because you promised to play a part here," Evan reminded him.

Scott shot him an icy gaze that the others didn't notice. "I am playing a part," Scott retorted. "You've seen what I brought to the table."

It was a week after Scott's arrival. When the men had met to plan their hunt, they had asked Scott what he had for guns and ammunition. He took them to the health station where he'd been staying and pulled a ring of keys from his waist to unlock one of the hard cases. A soft foam mould contained a 12-gauge pump-action shotgun, a .30-30 rifle, a smaller .22-calibre rifle, and two semi-automatic pistols. He lifted the holder to reveal a cache of ammunition. "Got enough here for when the shit really hits the fan," he explained with pride. Evan couldn't get Scott's artillery stock out of his mind.

"What's a zhaagnaash, anyway?" asked Scott. He pronounced the long vowels nasally and abruptly, and that made Isaiah and Jeff snicker.

"It's our traditional word for 'helpful friend,'" replied Evan.

"That's bullshit and you know it," grumbled Scott. The others just laughed. With his wide rawhide snowshoes on his feet, Dan, the elder of the group, led the way to the moose. Scott followed with his smaller metal ones, and Jeff walked beside him, sifting through the fresh snow in his traditional snowshoes. Evan and Isaiah walked back to where they had parked the snowmobiles to bring Scott's machine to the moose.

The three men stopped in front of the dead animal to marvel at his size. Their shadows loomed over the dead beast. "Fuckin' right we're gonna need my sled!" boasted Scott.

Dan frowned in annoyance as he pulled out a pouch of tobacco and pinched out a small amount. He elbowed Scott's forearm to get his attention to hand him the pouch. "Here, take this," Dan said. The beak of his hat concealed his eyes. "This is what we call semaa. It's tobacco. We make an offering to give thanks to this moose for offering its life to us."

"I've heard of this," Scott said, and he silently took the pouch and pinched some into his own hand. He handed it to Jeff, who did the same.

Dan took off his hat and began to pray. Jeff pulled back the hood of his parka and removed his ball cap and Scott pulled off his black toque when he saw what the others were doing. Dan finished the prayer with a miigwech and placed the tobacco in front of the dead moose with care and respect. Jeff followed, and Scott mimicked the motions of the others.

By the time Evan and Isaiah returned with the sleds, they were ready to lift the bull on and return to town. This is where Scott's muscle would come in handy. *He's pulling his weight,* thought Evan. *Maybe he'll be useful around here.*

TWENTY

Evan, Nicole, and their children dined under the yellow light-bulb that brightened the kitchen table. It was a moose roast with the last of the potatoes mashed for a side and heated canned corn. Evan was careful not to douse his potatoes with too much gravy. He wanted to savour them because no one knew when they'd be able to eat them again. He'd saved a few to plant in the spring, but he wasn't sure if they'd actually grow.

Cutlery clanked against thin glass plates as the family ate their meal with quiet chatter. They all took their time over the meal without the distraction of TV and homework. After supper, they unfolded worn board games, played cards, or told stories. The pace of their lives was slowing.

"Moozoo, that's moose," Nicole said to Maiingan. She took every opportunity to remind them of their Anishinaabemowin words. They had language classes at school, but there had been no regular classes for almost a month. The band couldn't justify using the fuel to keep the school open. Some teachers still held informal classes in their homes for families who wanted to maintain some kind of normal routine. But even those were happening less often. "Moozoo," the boy repeated.

"What's this?" Nicole asked, pointing at the corn on her plate. Maiingan stared at the vegetable, scrunching his face in concentration. "M . . . ma . . . man-daa-min?"

"Right! Mandaamin!" she said, holding out her hand for a high five. He slapped it with peak five-year-old force. "And that is?" she asked, pointing at the potatoes.

"Piniik!" he shouted. Nicole smiled and raised her palm for another celebratory slap.

The children were learning their language earlier and better than their parents had. Evan and Nicole had grown up in an era when Ojibwe wasn't spoken much with the younger generation at home. It was only two generations before Nicole and Evan that speaking Ojibwe was punished at the church-run schools that imprisoned stolen children, and the shame attached to it lingered. Evan and Nicole had vowed to make things different for their kids. They had given them Anishinaabemowin names with pride — Maiingan meant "wolf" and Nangohns "little star."

Evan gathered the empty plates and dropped them neatly into cold water in the sink. The council had asked everyone to shut off their hot water heaters the week before, and Evan had loyally heeded the request. Water for cooking or bathing was once again heated on the stovetop. Showers were gone, and a bath had become a twice-weekly routine. They'd likely have to reduce that even more if the rez wasn't going to run out of diesel before winter was over.

He cleared the pots and bowls of food, then put the leftovers into plastic containers and stacked them neatly in the fridge. He promised to wash the dishes when he got home later. He was off to check in on his brother to make sure he and his family had enough wood. Evan knew his little brother could easily become vulnerable and desperate.

He stood at the top of his steps in the dark of the early evening and let out a breath just to see the vapour billow from his mouth. He had done this since he was a kid to gauge the cold.

Thick clouds blocked the bright moon and the stars. The roads were blanketed in a darkness so heavy it was almost tangible. Evan drove along the white road he had recently ploughed. Most homes he passed were dark, save for one light in one window. It appeared the conservation message had finally sunk in: people were now complying — although, Evan felt not enough people understood the extent of their crisis. Perhaps the council should not have protected people so much at first. In recent weeks, he had silently begun to second-guess Terry's strategies and leadership. People weren't exactly rallying behind their chief, although most complied with his orders.

Evan pulled up to his brother's duplex. He noticed more lights on than usual. Smoke swirled out of the chimney. *At least he's burning wood and not using electric heat*, Evan thought. He walked up to the front door and knocked, although he usually just walked in. The crisis had put many people on edge, and he didn't want to alarm his brother. He was already at odds with Cam over his inactivity and lack of initiative. No need to make it worse.

No one came to the door. He heard muffled voices inside but couldn't tell who it was. He knocked again and waited. Still no one arrived to let him in, so he decided just to open the door and walk in after all.

A thick haze of cigarette smoke assaulted him. He had run

out of smokes a few days earlier, and the smoke stung his eyes though the longing remained. He heard loud chatter, the shouts and laughter of a small party. Bass-heavy music thumped from tiny speakers.

Evan was immediately annoyed, knowing that there would be more lights on and more toilet flushes than there should be. He took a deep breath and tried to contain his bubbling anger before walking into the kitchen.

Cam sat at the kitchen table with Nick Jones and his friend Jacob McCloud. Evan was surprised to see Nick, slightly younger than the other two and not generally a partier. "Hey bro!" Cam shouted, rising with arms outstretched. Greasy hair peeked out from under a toque, and his stained white T-shirt hung loosely off his skinny arms. He stumbled as he came towards Evan.

Evan let his younger brother wrap him in a drunken hug and squeezed him back before nudging him away. "How's it going, brother? Looks like you're nice and relaxed tonight," Evan said, barely containing his fury at his brother's fecklessness.

Cam stumbled back to his chair and shrugged. "Just survivin', bro," he said, cracking a wide, toothy smile.

A plastic bottle of rye was the table's centrepiece, an overflowing ashtray nestled up against it. Evan didn't recognize the brand of rye. It looked like it had been bought wholesale somewhere. He scanned the table and noticed the young men were drinking it straight. His jaw clenched, but he didn't want to alienate his brother's friends, so he moved to shake each of their hands.

"This is the fuckin' guy that saved my life!" slurred Nick. "These guys found us!"

Evan corrected him: "You guys found us."

"No way, man. I was so happy when I saw you guys there."

Evan didn't want to fall down this soggy, inebriated rabbit

hole. "I just came by to check on you guys," Evan said. He didn't see Sydney, but he heard more voices in the living room to his left. "You got enough wood?"

"Yep, for the whole winter," his brother replied, nodding his heavy, drunk head.

"What about food?"

"We just got our box for the week yesterday."

Evan had prepared it himself. He, Tyler, Isaiah, and a rotation of councillors delivered the food to prevent a pickup point from descending into mayhem as people got hungrier.

"Where's Jordan?"

"At Syd's mom's. We needed a night off. So I invited some people over."

"I see that. Where's Syd?"

Cam lifted his chin in the direction of the other room, pointing with his lips.

"Alright, I'll go in and say hi. Just remember to keep it down, and don't have too many lights on," he reminded the table. He knew he was in no position to cast stones about the drinking. He felt like indulging himself, but the sloppiness bothered him tonight, so he walked into the next room instead.

Light from a single lamp in the far corner illuminated the whole space. A tiny boom box beneath it played hip hop music. "Hey, Evan! Come over and have a drink!" shouted Sydney. That was the last thing he heard before blood rushed into his face and ears, drowning out sound.

Sitting in the opposite corner with Sydney's cousin Jenna on his lap was Scott. He raised his cup to Evan to salute his arrival. "Welcome, friend. Will you join us?"

Somehow Evan had known that the cigarettes and free-flowing booze would lead back to Scott. Scott hadn't been in the community long, but rumour had it that he was the man to go to if you'd run out of smokes or alcohol. He had somehow concealed a decent supply of vices in those hard cases he towed from the South. Desperate to keep his cool, Evan scanned the room. Sydney sat on the love seat to his left, leaning over the coffee table to knock the ash of her smoke into one of the empty red cups. Her younger sister Tara leaned back on the dark couch on the opposite side of the room closest to the light.

"What the fuck are you doing here?" he demanded through gritted teeth.

"Well, nice to see you too, friend," Scott replied sarcastically.

"I don't have time for your bullshit, Scott. What are you doing in my brother's house?"

"Your brother welcomed me in. I saw Nick by the band office the other day. He said they were having drinks here tonight. I figured I deserved to cut loose."

"Get your hands off the girl. She's too young for you."

"Evan, just chill out," Sydney muttered, rolling her glassy eyes.

Sensing the tension, Jenna stood up. "I gotta go pee," she said and made her way across the room. She flicked up her long black hair as she passed Evan. It smelled faintly sweet.

"Happy now?" Scott asked, his free hand clenched in a fist on his thigh. "I'm just here to make friends, Ev."

"I don't give a shit. You're too old for this crowd."

"Seriously, chill out, Evan," Sydney commanded.

"I'm not gonna chill out. This visitor has to respect our ways."

Scott's head snapped back in a fit of laughter, his big teeth catching the lamplight. "Your ways? You talk a big game about your so-called ways, Ev, but your brother tells me you enjoy the old firewater too."

Evan lurched towards Scott, his anger making him clumsy enough to knock cups off the coffee table. The bald man shot up to square up against him. They faced each other inches apart, staring each other down.

Scott leered into Evan's eyes and gritted his teeth, whispering, "Try it, tough guy" so that only Evan could hear. Even in the dim light Evan could see fading scars on the big man's forehead and cheek. He knew he was no match. *These useless fucks are all too drunk to back me up*, he thought as he took a step back.

Cam appeared in the doorway of the living room. "What's going on in here?"

"Ask your brother," said Scott.

Evan turned to look at his younger brother with a despairing affection. His face softened as he remembered just how naive and vulnerable Cam was. He remembered the sweet boy that he once was. He never really grew up. Soon his life would depend on it.

"Nothing, I was just heading out," said Evan. "Take care of each other."

He stepped around his brother and walked out of the house. He could hear Scott's booming laughter from inside as he opened the door to his truck.

TWENTY-ONE

He could barely hear the pounding on the front door from his burrow in the safe, warm confines of the bedroom but the boom reverberated through the house. A muffled voice yelled from outside and Evan jumped out of bed.

He rounded the corner and saw Isaiah standing at the door. Evan unlocked the bolt and let him in. "Izzy, what the fuck, man?"

Isaiah was trembling, the whites of his eyes gleaming in the pre-dawn darkness. "Get dressed. We gotta go," he said. "We got a real bad scene on our hands. I'll explain on the way."

Evan rushed back to the bedroom and looked for jeans and a sweater to put on over the long underwear he slept in.

"What's going on?" Nicole asked.

"Some kind of emergency," he said. "Izzy's here to take me somewhere."

"Damn. I hope everyone's okay,"

"Me too." He remembered the drunken scene at his brother's the night before and he was struck with foreboding. He rushed into his clothes and leaned over to kiss Nicole. "I'll be back as soon as I can to let you know what's up."

"Okay, be safe. I love you."

"I love you too."

He ran out to Isaiah's truck, threw open the door, and hopped in. They were peeling out of the driveway before he had a chance to shut the door.

"What's going on?" he huffed as Isaiah tore down the road.

"Fucked up news, man. Jenna and Tara Jones froze to death last night."

"What?"

"Yeah, Amanda found them in the ditch just down the road from her mom's place."

"Holy fuck."

"Yeah, I know. Terry and Amanda are both there. She went and got him. He got Walter, who came by my place to tell me to get you. Walter's figuring out what we're gonna do with the bodies."

Evan felt like he was sinking into the hard foam of the truck's seat. It took all his will not to heave up whatever was left in his stomach. "I saw them last night."

"What?"

"They were drinking at my brother's place. I stopped in there to check on him."

"Jesus Christ, man."

"Scott was there too."

It was the fastest drive through the rez Evan could remember.

Soon they were pulling up to a small cluster of trucks and people on the side of the road. The sun was clearing the horizon, blazing orange light into the grim ditch.

Terry, Amanda, and Walter watched their approach with stricken expressions. Evan wasn't quite ready to look at the bodies yet, so he put an arm around Amanda, who turned to give him a tight hug, her eyes bloodshot.

Evan steeled himself and stepped to the edge of the road. The two young women lay side by side in the ditch. Their brown faces were frozen blue and white. Tara's hood concealed most of her head, but Jenna's was down and her head was nestled into the snow with her long black hair splayed across her cousin's face. Evan remembered the fruity smell of her hairspray as she walked past him the night before. He looked at Tara and thought of Sydney. His heart broke for her.

"I don't know what they were doing." Amanda began to sob, grieving her young nieces. "They must have been walking home and just didn't make it all the way."

Terry turned to Evan. "It looks like they stuck to the road, wherever they were coming from."

Evan cleared his throat. "I know where they came from. They were drinking at my brother's place. I saw them there last night."

"What?" Amanda yelped.

"Yeah, I was worried about Cam's boy, so I stopped in to make sure they had food and wood. Except Jordan wasn't there. He was at Sydney's mom's. I guess they decided to have a party."

"Fuck sakes!" Terry stomped his foot and looked away.

Walter held up a hand. "Let's not jump to any conclusions yet. They musta got drunk and couldn't walk all the way home. We can't argue now. We gotta figure out where to take them before everyone gets up and sees us here."

The sun cut shadows across the snow. Soon it would shine

into the windows of the homes that lined the road, rousing the inhabitants for another day. Amanda began to cry again.

"Amanda, get in my truck," commanded Walter. "Terry, sit in there with her." When they were in the cab and out of earshot, he turned to Evan and Isaiah. "Right now, our only option is to take them to the health station. We have no way of getting anyone up here to do a fuckin' post mortem, and the ground's too frozen for a proper burial. So we'll have to keep them locked in the shed there while we sort all this shit out."

"Walter," Evan said. "Scott was there too."

"What?"

"Yeah, he was there drinking with them. You know they say that he's bootlegging the last of the booze."

"Jesus fucking Christ!"

"I know. I tried to get him to leave. But I couldn't. He wouldn't listen to me."

"Fuck. We'll deal with that later too. Come on, help me get these girls ready."

Walter had driven to the health station earlier, while Isaiah had gone to get Evan, but he didn't know where to find the body bags. He had gone back to his own home to get old dark blankets he had stored away. He walked to the back of his truck to grab them and handed Evan and Isaiah three each.

"I don't know how we're supposed to do this," admitted Isaiah, "but we should at least offer some semaa, I think." He dug a pouch out of his jacket and passed it awkwardly to the other men. They prayed silently and put it down close to where the young women lay. They dug their stiff bodies out of the snow, wrapped them carefully, and carried them one at a time to Isaiah's truck, placing them gently on the open truck bed. Evan stayed in the back with Tara and Jenna while Isaiah drove to their temporary resting place in the shed behind the health station.

Terry met Walter, Evan, and Isaiah at the shed after driving Amanda home. He stepped out of his red pickup, looking defeated. *I gotta tell him right away*, thought Evan.

"Hey, Terry, there's something you should know about last night . . ." The front door of the band office swung open. It was Scott, outfitted in his snowmobile gear, holding his black helmet.

"Good morning, boys," he bellowed. "To what do I owe this esteemed visit?"

"Not now, Scott," Terry muttered.

"Oh? What's up?"

"Please, just give us a few minutes."

Scott shrugged but stayed where he was.

Evan stepped closer to the chief. "Terry," he whispered, as close as he could stand to him. "Scott was with them last night."

Terry squinted his eyes in chagrin. "What? With who?"

"With the girls. He was at my brother's place last night too."

"Well, what the fuck happened then?"

"I don't know."

Terry looked over Evan's shoulder at Scott. "Goddamn it, Evan, who else was there?"

"Other than Cam and Syd, Nick and Jacob."

"Nick Jones?"

"Well, where is he? And Jacob?"

Evan's heart skipped a beat. He hadn't given them a thought. They likely would have left his brother's place sometime in the night as well, and he had no idea if they made it home.

In the still, frigid air, the faint hum of snowmobiles interrupted them. It had been weeks since anyone had ridden their machines for leisure, so the sound from the south was unmistakable. Now they were used only for hunting or running crisis errands.

Evan peered at Scott. Scott looked at Isaiah, whose eyes

darted to Walter. Walter awaited a signal from the chief. "Where's that coming from?" he thought aloud when it became clear that Terry wasn't going to do anything.

"I think we have some visitors," said Scott calmly. "My bet's on the hydro line."

"We have to go head them off," said Walter, wearily taking control. "Isaiah, you stay here with the girls. Scott, get in with me. Evan, jump in Terry's truck."

The trucks roared down the hill, took a left, and went straight to the store. Four machines were approaching. They staggered the two trucks to create a makeshift blockade, although anyone looking to bypass it on a snowmobile could easily take the ditch around. Walter and Terry left their trucks running as everyone got out.

The snowmobiles neared the ridge that marked the end of the ploughed road, slowed, and slid down, stopping a safe distance from the men and the trucks. They formed a line. The second rider from the right in a dark red and black suit raised his gloved hands in a peaceful gesture. The others did the same. The man turned off his engine, stepped off his snowmobile, and walked towards the waiting men with his hands still raised.

He looked to be a large man, a little bigger than Walter. He put down his arms, and they swished against his snowmobile jacket. His heavy boots clunked against the hard ground.

The two to the left got off their machines, and the leader took off his helmet. His tousled blond hair glowed in the morning sun. His face was pale, with a square jaw and high cheekbones.

"Hello, hi . . ." he began, as his voice cracked. "Where are we?"

"Gaawaandagkoong First Nation. Who are you?" Terry responded.

"We've been travelling a long time. We started in Everton Mills. We're so hungry."

Everton Mills was a small city farther south than Gibson. Evan surveyed their machines and couldn't see any sleds attached with any indication of supplies.

"If you came that far," Walter asked, "then where's all your gear?"

"We set up camp about an hour's drive south of here yesterday. We're desperate to find anyone else. Please, do you have any food?"

He held his helmet in one arm, and Evan noticed his free hand trembling. There was fear, and desperation, in his eyes. The other newcomers started walking towards them.

"We have food," said Terry, "for our community. You can appreciate that we're hungry here too."

"Please," the man said. "We're starving."

The three behind him wobbled where they stood. They looked weak.

"You'll need to cooperate," Terry continued. "Who are you?"

"My name's Phillips."

"Do you have a first name, Phillips?"

"Mark."

"Mark, how do we know there aren't more people on sleds waiting behind you to swarm us?"

"You have my word."

"I don't know what your word is worth."

"I'm begging you," Phillips pounded his fist against his thigh.

"I'm asking for your patience," Terry said firmly. "We're a small community. We're already stretched thin."

"Let us by!" Phillips screamed and suddenly charged towards Terry. Four sharp cracks rang out and the stranger crumpled to the ground. The woman screamed and the men rushed forward. Phillips rolled on the road, groaning and bleeding into the snow.

· 140 ·

Scott held his handgun tightly with both hands, pointing at the remaining three.

"Stay back! Stay back!" he commanded. Everyone stared at him in disbelief.

"Now you fuckin' listen to this chief!" Scott ordered. "No quick moves! If you want to come in here, it's on our terms!" On the ground before them, Phillips stopped moving. The woman retreated back to the snowmobiles and wailed.

Terry took a few steps toward Scott. "Jesus, Scott," he whispered through his teeth. "What the fuck?"

"There'll be more coming, Terry," he responded. "We gotta make a stand." He kept his pistol pointed at the others.

"You didn't have to shoot him. You had no right to shoot him. You're an outsider here, too, remember."

"He was desperate and crazy. I was protecting us."

"What are we gonna do with the others now?"

Shit, Terry's lost control, thought Evan. *He just handed it over to Scott.*

"We gotta screen them. That Phillips was obviously their leader."

"And what do we do now with Phillips?"

"Put him at the end of the road there. As a warning."

Scott holstered his handgun and walked back to the truck. Walter and Evan stared at each other in stunned disbelief. Terry looked at his boots. Phillips bled out on the snow.

PART TWO

BIBOON

WINTER

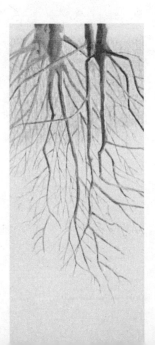

TWENTY-TWO

Evan rummaged through the old man's closet, feeling for heavy winter jackets, or at least thick wool. The dark, damp basement already reeked of mould and, as he reached deeper into the garments, the scent of mothballs danced with the must in his nostrils. He felt a coarse jacket and pulled it out into the faint daylight coming through the small window above his head. It was a formal military blazer. He recognized it from Remembrance Day ceremonies and grand entries at powwows. He remembered the old man looking proud and mighty every time he put it on.

But here, in this lonely, near-empty basement, it looked stiff and rotting. Evan held it higher for a better look. The blue wool had faded and felt thin. He noticed that the buttons on the sleeves and the breast weren't actually gold as he had always thought as a child. They were brass and tarnished. He ran his calloused fingertip across the three smaller ones on the jacket's left wrist, feeling the bumps and grooves of the tiny crests. He pictured the old man holding the eagle staff proudly, wearing this military garb. The buttons' golden charm had seemed to accentuate the flags and feathers on the ceremonial stave.

But they no longer shone. They never did, really. Evan wondered if Remembrance Day would ever happen again.

The wood furnace in the middle of the room blasted heat that dissipated as it reached the unfinished concrete walls. He replaced the jacket and closed the closet door, then fed another five pieces of wood into the furnace. Isaiah would come later in the evening to feed the fire again for the old lady.

Aileen was sitting at the kitchen table, sipping from the tea she had promised Evan. She still had an old wood cookstove in her kitchen and she could handle keeping it stoked, but she was too frail now to load the furnace in the basement. The main floor was toasty and it comforted Evan to know that Aileen was okay. He took off his jacket and placed it on the back of the wooden chair across from the elder. She put down her cup and smiled at him through her big glasses. "Everything okay down there?" she asked. Evan looked down at the full cup in front of him, then to hers. She had wrapped her thin, wrinkled fingers around the hot glass for warmth. The sleeves of her pink sweater were fraying at the end.

"Yeah, everything looks good. You got lots of wood still," he replied. "Izzy will be by tonight to top it up."

"I really appreciate you boys doing this for me. Chimiigwech."

"It's nothing, Auntie. We're happy to help."

Aileen was the last of the generation raised speaking

Anishinaabemowin, with little English at all. She was one of only a few dozen left who could speak their language fluently. She remembered the old ways and a lot of the important ceremonies. She had more knowledge than everyone else about the traditional lives of the Anishinaabeg.

"Aaniish ezhebimaadziiyin?" he asked.

"Mino ya. I'm warm. I have lots to eat. I get a lot more company these days."

"That's good. We want to make sure everything's okay around here."

"How are you doing?"

He paused. He couldn't remember the last time someone had asked him that. His pace had been frenetic in the strange darkness of this new era. "I'm, uh, good, I guess."

"How are the kids?"

"Oh, they're good. They've been spending a lot of time outside. I don't think they miss school at all!" he chuckled, and she giggled.

"What about your bazgim?"

"Oh, she's tired, but she's getting by. She really appreciates all the things you are teaching her about the old medicine ways, but she still gets stuck at home a lot with the kids while I'm out here doing stuff."

"Well, you make sure you spend some time with her. Go for a walk in the bush. When the spring comes, ask her to show you some of the medicines. She'll know a lot now, if she remembers all the stuff from when I used to take her and all the young girls out there. It will be important if we don't get any new supplies in from the hospital down south."

Evan thought of Nicole at home, trying to prepare herself for the skills they would need if the power was gone for good while struggling to keep the children occupied. He felt a twinge of guilt. She often looked tired these days. She didn't talk as much as she used to and hardly smiled anymore. No one smiled much this winter.

"That's a good idea," he said. "Maybe I'll take the kids over to my parents' place tomorrow or the day after."

"Your mom will appreciate the kookom time."

"Yeah, for sure."

He brought the hot tea to his chapped lips and sipped. The liquid seeped into the cracks and burned, but he showed no reaction. He'd learned to keep his thoughts behind a careful mask. He could not show weakness, especially now. But the old woman could still make him smile.

"Did you find anything down there in Eddie's closet?" she asked.

"I found one of his old army jackets, but I didn't wanna take it."

"The one he wore for ceremonies?"

"Yeah, that one."

"Ah yes. He loved that one." She looked out the window.

Her husband had served in the Korean War and had been the last wartime military veteran in the community. He had died four years ago, disappointed that no young people had followed in his path. He had been celebrated as a strong warrior and a respected elder. Evan thought about him now, wondering if he would have been able to help guide the young people through this catastrophe if he were still alive.

Evan sipped the tea slowly. There was no need to fill the silence. *If we can make it through this winter*, Evan thought, *we'll be okay*.

Often, Aileen shared a teaching or an old story with the young men when they came to visit. Once in a while, someone would bring a group of children or teens to hear some old Nanabush stories or her memories of the old days. There had been no electricity in this community when she was a child and parents sometimes brought the young ones to her to remind them that life was possible without the comforts of modern technology. Now it was critical that they learn how the old ones lived on the land.

"You know, when young people come over, sometimes some of them talk about the end of the world," Aileen said, breaking the silence and snapping Evan out of his woolgathering. He looked up from the plaid pattern on the vinyl tablecloth to the old woman's face.

"They say that this is the end of the world. The power's out and we've run out of gas and no one's come up from down south. They say the food is running out and that we're in danger. There's a word they say too — ah . . . pock . . . ah . . ."

"Apocalypse?"

"Yes, apocalypse! What a silly word. I can tell you there's no word like that in Ojibwe. Well, I never heard a word like that from my elders anyway."

Evan nodded, giving the elder his full attention.

"The world isn't ending," she went on. "Our world isn't ending. It already ended. It ended when the Zhaagnaash came into our original home down south on that bay and took it from us. That was our world. When the Zhaagnaash cut down all the trees and fished all the fish and forced us out of there, that's when our world ended. They made us come all the way up here. This is not our homeland! But we had to adapt and luckily we already knew how to hunt and live on the land. We learned to live here."

She became more animated as she went on. Her small hands swayed as she emphasized the words she wanted to highlight. "But then they followed us up here and started taking our children away from us! That's when our world ended again. And that wasn't the last time. We've seen what this . . . what's the word again?"

"Apocalpyse."

"Yes, apocalypse. We've had that over and over. But we always survived. We're still here. And we'll still be here, even if the power and the radios don't come back on and we never see any white people ever again."

Evan gazed back down to the table. He felt his shoulders ease and his chest open up. He was tired, but she gave him hope. "You're right, Auntie," he said. "I never thought of it that way."

He smiled, and she smiled back, crow's feet creasing at the corners of her eyes.

"Well, I should probably head back out there," he said, as he tipped back the cup into his mouth.

"Okay then. Busy day?"

"Not really. Just gotta tie up some loose ends." He didn't want to tell her the morbid details of his next task. He got up and put on his jacket and zipped it up. He took the black toque out of his right pocket and pulled it over his shaggy black hair, which nearly hung into his eyes. He said miigwech and smiled before walking out the back door.

His sturdy yellow snowshoes were propped up against the porch. Evan sat on the step and, his hands bare, threaded the leather straps through the metal buckles at the heels and toes of both feet. He lifted each foot and shook it to ensure the shoe was snug.

He shoed around to the front of the house and through the deep snow on the driveway. The snow continued to fall, as it had for days, whiting out nearly everything, save for the homes and the trees that were tall enough to rise above the snowline. He looked back at Aileen's house one more time and saw her in the large picture window, waving. He smiled and waved back. The smoke coming from the chimney put him at ease. She would be okay for another day.

He walked onto the road, now devoid of trucks and cars.

Once the diesel supply became critically low, the ploughs had stopped running. Most of the town's trucks and cars had run out of gas anyway. Within a few days of steady snowfall, the roads had become impassable.

Two weeks earlier, the diesel had finally run out. It came as little surprise to most. Still, it had resulted in a handful of frustrated people storming the shop to demand some sort of solution, still clinging to the idea that other people could fix their problems.

In reality, there was a small amount of diesel left for one last burst — to boost the generators to reconnect to the hydro grid, if it came back online, or to fuel up vehicles once again for some sort of voyage somewhere to get supplies or connect with another community to consolidate resources. Either possibility seemed remote.

So Evan was now doing his rounds on foot, checking in on the elderly, or those who needed help keeping their fires burning or making food. He didn't really have an official job anymore. The band administration had essentially dissolved, save for organizing weekly food handouts from the cache. Some people still saw Terry and the rest of the council as the figureheads of the community, but their influence was greatly diminished. Walter was the one council member most people now turned to if they needed a problem solved. And Walter, in turn, relied on Evan, Isaiah, and Tyler. Otherwise, people had retreated to their family groups or had now fallen under the spell of Justin Scott's promises of easier living under his authority. Alliances were forming and shifting, and Evan was uneasy.

The hypnotic crunch of his steps was the only sound he heard on this still day. The afternoon chill was deep and people kept indoors if they could. Grey smoke pumped from each chimney.

The crust of the snow he broke was thicker than his

snowshoes. He kicked up frozen shrapnel each time he raised a foot. A fine powder lay underneath. The conditions made him think of the specific time of year. *There's a word for this,* he thought, trying to remember with each high step across the hard snow. His knees raised as if to rev his mind into higher gear. He looked up to the lumpy clouds in the hope that the word would emerge like a ray of sunlight through overcast sky.

"Onaabenii Giizis," he proudly proclaimed out loud. "The moon of the crusted snow." His words fell flat on the white ground in front of him and he wondered which month that actually was.

Onaabenii Giizis usually referred to February but it could also apply to early March. He remembered hearing two teachers dispute about it when he was younger. One of them was convinced it meant the time at the peak of winter when the weather was so cold the snow simply froze over. The other said it was later in the season when the weather fluctuated between freezing and milder temperatures, causing the snow to melt and then freeze again, creating a crust.

Evan thought it must still be deep winter and that this crust he was walking through was what the first teacher from his memory was talking about. There had been no mild weather yet. The deep freeze was unrelenting. The wind howled. Blizzards continued to blow in. There were calm, sunny days of bearable temperatures, but otherwise there was no real respite from the harshest of seasons here in the North. The crusted snow moon sounded severe to him. He agreed with the first teacher. *This must be the peak of Onaabenii Giizis,* he thought.

He had stopped counting the days and weeks long ago. There was no point anymore knowing if it was Tuesday the twenty-first of whatever. All that mattered was getting through each season and preparing for the next.

Now the milestones he used to mark time were the deaths in the community. The toll was rising steadily as people perished through sickness, mishap, violence, or by their own hands. Even in a place as familiar with tragedy as a northern reserve, it had reached levels he had never experienced.

Evan's trips to the band office, the elders' homes he served, and back home had become routine. He had trained himself to think deliberately, to ponder things that settled his mind. He thought about spots where they could gather more wood. He reviewed rabbit snare knots. He visualized pulling back an arrow and letting it fly at a target. He had discovered that reviewing routines in his head helped him keep desperation at bay. As long as the wind didn't blow too harshly and the snowfall abated, he even enjoyed these walks.

He trudged up to the side of the garage at the band office. He opened the heavy green door that was never locked anymore and propped it open with a grey cinder block to let in some meagre light. He stepped inside and went right to the chains that opened the garage door manually. He pulled down, and it slowly lifted, letting in a sliver of white daylight underneath. A few more solid yanks of the chain and the door was up, illuminating the garage behind him. He ignored the rows of bodies wrapped in blankets and bags and stepped back outside to await the others.

Two figures appeared on the hill in the distance, pulling a sled. Evan recognized his friends by their walk, even in snowshoes. They were immersed in conversation, making animated hand gestures. The two young men had become accustomed to their grim task as makeshift undertakers.

The plastic sled scraped loudly against the hard snow, drowning out their voices as they neared. Its heavy cargo dug into the crusty chunks and powder, sinking in slightly. The two seemed to ignore it as they greeted Evan.

"Hey, Ev, get a load of this fuckin' guy," said Isaiah. "He figures Toronto woulda been in a playoff spot by now."

"Fuckin' right they woulda been," said Tyler. "They had the hottest start ever! And if they kept it up, playoffs would be starting pretty soon."

"Well, one of you is full of shit, that's for sure," Evan smiled, shaking his head. "But I guess we'll never know who."

"Just watch, all this shit's gonna come back on, and they'll be in the playoffs. They probably been playing this whole time, and we just been in the dark," said Tyler. He had been one of the best young players on the reserve and had been scouted for a junior team in Gibson when he was fifteen. But there was a blizzard the day he was supposed to fly down, stranding him on the reserve, and the opportunity never arose again.

Despite Tyler's optimism, Evan doubted the lights would ever come back on. *Hockey as we know it is done*, he thought. He shook off that notion and focused on the job they had to do: today it was Johnny Meegis they would lay to rest in the garage.

"So how was it, getting old Johnny here?" Evan asked, jutting his chin towards the black body bag on the sled. It was difficult for him to square the long black lump before him with his mental image of the elder.

Isaiah twisted to look back at the sled. "He was pretty stiff by the time we got there," he said. "We had trouble getting him into the bag."

"All his kids and grandkids were there," said Tyler. "They were all pretty upset. It was a rough scene."

"Do they know what happened to him?" asked Evan.

"They think it was his heart, or his diabetes."

"Probably a combination of things," added Isaiah, matter-of-factly. He was never one to reveal much emotion.

"Yeah, I guess we won't really know," stated Tyler. "Too bad, anyways."

They left it at that and pulled the sled into the garage. It was a tragic routine the three had been assigned earlier in the winter, and it had become one of their primary jobs now that there wasn't any more ploughing to do. When word got around that there was a death, it was up to them to collect the body and bring it here to the garage, where it would wait out the winter. The community would bury their loved ones after the spring thaw.

Evan squatted at the head of the body and slid his hands underneath the shoulders. Tyler positioned himself to pick up the legs. They gave each other a quick nod and heaved upwards. Evan took a few steps backward and to his left, and they carefully placed Johnny beside Mark Whitesky, Evan's older cousin who had frozen to death not far from his house a few days earlier. Evan hadn't decided if he thought his cousin had had an accident or if he had killed himself by walking out into the cold.

After they had settled Johnny, they surveyed the room to ensure everything was as they left it last time. The makeshift morgue housed twenty-one bodies lined neatly in three rows. Johnny Meegis closed out the third. The garage had room for at least three more, and they could squeeze in more with some rearranging. But with each body, the three friends hoped it would be the last.

In the back left corner lay young Jenna and Tara Jones, the first to go. Their bodies were moved here after the leaders had come to the grim realization that there would be more deaths over the winter and that they would need somewhere cold to keep them until spring.

Soon after, Jacob McCloud was found hanging from a tree in the bush behind his parents' house. Friends said that he'd been overwhelmed by the guilt of letting the young women walk home drunk on a frigid night. They'd been his close friends. His body lay beside theirs. But dispute lingered over what exactly had happened to the girls. Word trickled through the rez that Scott somehow got hostile that night, but when asked about it, Cam and Sydney either wouldn't talk about it or they'd say they didn't remember. Scott had allies on the rez now and it was hard to get answers. He and his cronies lived in the duplexes that had been abandoned when families began consolidating as the blackout wore on.

Next to Jacob's body, wrapped in old, tattered blue sheets, was his cousin, Dion McCloud. He had shot himself a few days later, near the tree where Jacob had died. One suicide often led to another among the young people, and the compounding tragedies squeezed the stammering heart of the reserve.

In the next row were mostly people who had died of natural causes. Many were elderly. Johnny Meegis was neatly lined up with the rest of them.

"Journey well, Johnny," said Tyler.

"He's definitely on his way to a better place than this," muttered Isaiah. "We don't gotta do anything else, do we?"

"You said they had a ceremony at his house?" asked Evan.

"Yeah."

"Nah, I don't think we gotta do anything. Just pay your respects on your own, I guess."

Isaiah and Tyler nodded silently.

"Might as well go home."

Evan pulled at the chains to shut the large garage door, shrouding the bodies once again in darkness. He knew they'd be back, likely sooner than later.

TWENTY-THREE

Nicole looked out the front window at the still trees and the settled snow. It looked calm. She opened the door and took a step halfway out to gauge the temperature. It felt relatively mild, given the frigid weather they'd endured so far this winter. It seemed like a good afternoon to take the kids for a walk.

She bundled up Maiingan and Nangohns and sat them on the front porch while she put on her snowshoes to walk around the house to get the wooden sleigh from under the back steps. The thin wooden straps of the basket were blistered and worn, but its long skis slid smoothly across the thick snow. It still seemed to work well, but Nicole wondered how much her son and daughter would weigh it down.

"Aambe maajaadaa, binoojiinyag," she said. "Let's go, kiddies."

The boy bounded down the stairs, while Nangohns hesitated. She whined as she saw her brother take a seat at the front of the sleigh. Her pleas verged on tears before her mother decided to step in.

"Give your sister the front," she commanded. "You're taller. You can see over her head."

He shimmied back in his thick blue snow pants to let his sister onto the sleigh. She nestled in for the ride as Nicole called out, "Okay, you guys ready?"

With the leather strap wrapped around her thick deer-hide mitts, Nicole tugged at the sleigh. It moved easily across the snow; the load of children felt a lot lighter than she expected. *Maybe we'll go a little farther then*, she thought.

The thick cloud cover insulated them from the stinging air of a clear, windy day. It reminded Nicole that there would be an end to this season, as there always was. At times, though, she wasn't so certain. Everything was different. Things they had come to rely on had fallen apart and their community had been turned upside down. There were days when she wasn't sure if she was awake or dreaming.

But this was real, and she was sure of it. She was sure of her children's warm skin and beating hearts. She had felt their breath close to her as she dressed them for this trip outdoors. She was determined that they would survive and thrive on this land, despite the building sickness and despair around them. She turned to look behind her. "You guys doing okay?"

"Yeah, Mommy."

"Okay, good. We'll just go a little bit down the road. Maybe we'll go see Grandma and Grandpa."

That meant her parents. Evan's parents were known by the Ojibwe words for grandfather and grandmother — mishomis and nookomis (or kookom, which was interchangeable) — while

Gary and Theresa McCloud went by the English words. It was really just to differentiate the sets of grandparents, although there was some logic to it, given that Dan and Patricia spoke more of the language in their home.

Up the road, Nicole noticed someone crouched over in the ditch, digging at something. She could only make out a blue figure, but as they approached she recognized Meghan Connor, the sole woman from the group of refugees who had come after Scott.

Meghan heard the sleigh on the snow and stood up to see them coming. "Hey there."

"Hi," replied Nicole. "Staying warm?"

"Yeah, I'm just checking on some rabbit snares. No luck so far."

Nicole scanned the snow-covered ditch in both directions. "I don't think the rabbits make burrows this close to the road. It might be a while before they come back this way."

"Oh, right. This used to be the road. I forgot." Meghan readjusted her wool toque while she looked down at the snow to hide her embarrassment.

"Where's the rest of your crew?"

"The other guys went to check more traps. They're all spread around."

"You guys got enough to eat over there?"

"Yeah, I think so. Haven't been too hungry yet anyway."

The days after the second wave of newcomers arrived had been tense and awkward. After Scott had killed one of the refugees, Terry and Walter had felt obliged to take them in — though they hadn't been planning to turn them away. They moved quickly to house the three surviving members of the group in Walter's basement while they made arrangements for more long-term housing.

Brad, his wife Meghan, and the third man, Alex Richer,

mourned their friend while they settled in to their new reality. Walter and his wife did what they could to make them feel at home, cooking moose and deer and sharing stories about the community and the people who lived there. All three helped with chopping and piling wood and cooking. Eventually Brad and Alex joined Walter when he set and checked rabbit snares.

After a month, the newcomers had moved into the row of duplex bungalows. While many of the original inhabitants had moved in with other family, some remained there, including Cam. Nicole pictured the row of brown duplex homes and wondered whether the bush on that end of the community yielded enough wildlife to feed these white people. She also wondered how well they knew how to trap.

Meghan stepped up from the dip where the ditch used to be. Her narrow aluminum snowshoes sank slightly into the crust of the snow. She smiled at the children in the wooden sled. "Hi there, what are your names?"

"I'm Maiingan, and this my sister Nangohns," the boy said.

"Aaniin!" the girl piped up from the front.

"Those are nice names!"

"We were going a little stir-crazy in the house all morning," said Nicole. "I decided to take them out for some fresh air."

"That's a good idea. At least it's not windy out today."

Nicole noticed Meghan's gaunt cheeks and the heavy purple circles shadowing her bright blue eyes. It shocked Nicole, who remembered her looking healthier. She couldn't remember the last time she had seen her, though. Most people just let the visitors be in the small pocket the community had granted them.

"You're Nicole, right? Evan's wife?"

"Sort of. We were planning on eventually making it official but all this happened. And I know you're Meghan."

"I guess pretty much everyone around here knows our names, eh? There's no hiding."

"Well, if anyone can hide in the snow, it's you guys."

Meghan let out a nervous chuckle.

"I'm just kidding," assured Nicole.

They both giggled. Then Meghan held her stomach and leaned over in uncontrollable laughter. She caught her breath and stood up. "Sorry," she said. "I guess I needed that."

Nicole guessed Meghan was a little older than her, but not by much. But she had aged. She looked malnourished, exhausted, and even traumatized. And Nicole knew who was the root of that trauma. She felt sympathy but wasn't sure if she wanted to connect with this woman, or how to do it while staying out of Scott's way.

"Sometimes all we got is laughter," Nicole said, echoing something her own mother would say. "Around here we say it's good medicine."

"Not much to laugh about these days, though."

"You guys are still settling in. It'll get better." Nicole's words hung in the air. She sensed the woman in front of her was on the verge of breaking. "Are you really alright over in your new place?"

"As good as we can be, I guess."

Meghan paused and Nicole waited. It was obvious to her there was more this tired woman wanted to say.

"Scott's a fucking asshole," Meghan blurted out. "Sorry for swearing in front of your kids."

"Don't worry. They've heard them all by now. Especially since winter started." Nicole flashed a friendly half-smile to ease the other woman's rising tension and noticed tiny tears threatening to slip from Meghan's eyes.

"He just . . . he orders us around. He threatens us. And the worst part is, Brad has totally fallen in line."

"That's your husband?"

"Yeah. It's like he's his little lapdog. And sometimes I catch Scott staring at me. It really creeps me out. I'm worried he's gonna . . ."

Her voice cracked before trailing off. Nicole stepped forward to put her hand on her shoulder. Meghan tensed up at first, then Nicole felt her ease.

"Do you want to come back to our place for some tea and something to eat?"

Meghan wiped her nose with the back of her glove and sniffled hard. "Thanks, but I better not. I have more snares to check. He's expecting us to bring back some food."

"Is he pulling his weight at least?"

"I really don't know. He says he has a plan."

"A plan for what?"

"A plan for stuff to eat whenever all that emergency food runs out."

"What could that be? We're hunting and trapping already. We'll set nets for fish when the ice breaks up."

"He says that won't do it. He always nods at Brad and Alex when that comes up — like he's trying to intimidate them. But they won't say anything to me about it. And it's weird — he seems to be getting bigger, though I know that's not possible. Probably it's just the rest of us are getting skinnier."

Nicole felt a chill run through her arms. *What's he planning on eating?* she wondered. "Do you think they're —"

"Sorry, I gotta go," Meghan interrupted. "They're probably waiting for me."

"No, wait, just come get warm for a few minutes."

"No, I can't. Thanks, though. I'll see you around. Nice to meet you kids!" She turned and trudged through the snow as quickly as the snowshoes would let her.

"Wait, hold up . . . Meghan!"

Her back was to them as she threw up a hand to wave goodbye. The emptiness in her gut told Nicole to take the kids back home.

TWENTY-FOUR

Tyler fumbled with a heavy ring of keys as dawn broke in the east. The cold bit at his bare fingers. Terry, Evan, and Isaiah stood behind him, shuffling on the crusty snow with their snowshoes under their arms.

"Goddamn it, hurry up!" prodded Isaiah. "It's fuckin' freezing out here!"

"Calm your ass down," Tyler responded. "I got it."

Keys clanked as he unlocked and pulled the door to the shop open. They entered, their billowing breath tinted purple and orange in the morning light.

Ration day was Tuesday. Though most had abandoned their calendars, they managed to count the days between the rationing. Terry still managed the food dispersal and he maintained a routine as best he could. He relied on a small black day planner that he kept in the front pocket of his parka, but it wouldn't matter if he lost it: the hungry showed up every Tuesday, earlier and earlier with each passing week.

Home delivery of food supplies had ended about two months earlier, when the gas and diesel allotted for vehicles ran out. Now it was up to each person to come and get their own rations. The shop had become the designated pickup spot because of the bodies stored in the garage at the band office. It was farther for most people to walk, but it was the only reasonable solution. Few other community buildings were fortified or secure.

Late one night, they had moved about half of the food cache — enough for the rest of the winter, they calculated — from its storage under the garage to the shop. It took all night. With the bodies lying nearby, the process was sombre and weird.

Isaiah went to the back room to start a fire in the backup wood furnace. The brightening morning pushed through the small windows on the east and north walls of the building, lighting the main room where the men gathered. Each sat on a plastic chair, waiting for the space to warm before getting to work.

"We gonna have any major meltdowns today?" Evan asked.

"Hope not," said Terry.

Roughly 100 people came every week for food. When you multiplied that with the number of people back in their homes that was about a quarter of the community's population. The others still had enough, with their own stockpiles of frozen meat and canned food gathered and bought before the blackout in the fall.

Evan and Tyler went to the back to get boxes of canned ham and peas and hauled them to the front, placing them behind the white tables that would become the weekly dole station. They repeated this until they had eight hundred cans ready to go.

"I dunno how these people can eat this shit," muttered Tyler, setting down a case of canned ham. It was a generic brand, also known as "rez food." Only the most impoverished ate it — those with a little more money or hunting and fishing skills took pride in being able to avoid it. But now, few could afford to be picky.

"I dunno man, fry it up and put some mustard on it, and it's not too bad," said Evan.

"That's sick."

"What kind of snob are you, anyway? Don't forget, you're rez, man!"

"Yeah, but until everything goes back to normal, I can take care of myself."

"What do you mean 'back to normal'?"

"When the power's back on and everything."

Evan said nothing. He couldn't tell if his friend was naïve or in denial. He thought it was likely the latter: maybe it was the trauma of his younger brother Kevin's story of escaping the collapse of the city. Maybe Tyler just didn't want to accept it.

When they returned with the last of the cans for the week, Amanda was at the table, poring over a handwritten chart and making an inventory of what was going out. The front door opened again, letting a blast of cold air in, and Sydney, Cam's partner, walked in. "Mino gizheb. How you guys doing this morning?"

Amanda looked up at her niece and smiled. "Oh hi, my girl! Nice to see you. We're doing good, thanks. You here for some miijim?"

"Yeah, if you got some." She pulled two large canvas bags out of her parka pockets and walked up to the table. "Miigwech, I really appreciate it."

"How's my nephew doing?" Evan asked.

"Oh, he's good. He loves being with his grandma and grandpa all the time now."

That was news to Evan. "He's with your mom and dad?" he asked. He knew they stayed there regularly, but this sounded permanent.

"Yeah. I am too."

"How long you been there?"

"Almost a week now."

"Oh yeah? How come?"

"I didn't want Jordan to be around those people anymore."

Scott and his followers. The rumours had only grown since their last confrontation. Evan realized, with a jolt and some shame, that he had been avoiding his brother. Sydney's stern tone and blank face scared and disturbed him.

"Is Cam with you at your parents'?" he asked.

"He drops in once in a while," she replied, as she helped Amanda load her bags with the cans.

"What do you mean?"

"You should probably find your brother and talk to him."

Sensing the tension rising, Amanda changed the topic. "Do you guys have any flour left over at your mom and dad's?"

"Yeah, a couple bags."

"You should probably use it up soon. Do you know how old it is? It might start going bad. Fry up some bread and freeze it for later. These cans won't keep you full."

"Okay, thanks, Auntie. Yeah, I made some bannock, but I also got some bags of it frozen too. I'll do the rest today."

She picked up the heavy bags in each hand, and turned back to the door.

"Do you need a hand with that?" Evan asked.

Sydney turned to look at him. "No, I'm good thanks. It's a good workout. It's gonna be beach season again soon so I gotta stay in shape." She chuckled and smiled at him, but the smile didn't reach her eyes. He remembered her younger sister Tara, frozen in the ditch months earlier.

"Bring Nic and the kids by my mom and dad's place some-time," she said.

"For sure, that'd be nice."

"K, see you guys later."

Evan watched her leave and thought about his brother. *What the hell is he up to?* he thought. *Is he hanging around Scott? He should really know better.*

"Hey, I think there's a couple more boxes we gotta get." Isaiah broke into Evan's reverie and motioned to the back of the shop. Evan followed Isaiah through the door and into the dark storage area, where Isaiah turned to him with a worried look. "What she said reminded me of something."

"What's that?"

"I saw Nick on the road yesterday afternoon when I was going from Candace's to my dad's."

"Oh yeah? What was he doing?"

The disastrous party at Cam's flashed into Evan's mind. Since then he had rarely seen his younger brother's friend.

"He didn't look good."

"Really?"

"No, he was kind of pale. He looked real skinny. His cheeks were sunken in."

"Is he sick?"

"Maybe. Maybe he's just hungry."

"Weird. Why isn't he out snaring rabbits? Why doesn't his uncle share his stash of food with him at least? Donny should have enough if he has the Northern's inventory squirrelled away like they say."

Isaiah shrugged. "He said something really weird to me too."

"Oh yeah? What?"

"He said that he had just seen Scott walking down the road."

The mere mention of the man made Evan's fingers curl into fists.

Isaiah continued. "He said that Scott stopped him and started asking him weird questions, like about how hungry he was. He said Scott had told him that he knew where to get extra food if he needed it."

"What the hell?"

"Yeah, he said then Scott tried to get him to go with him. He said he almost went, but he got creeped out. He was walking back home when I saw him."

"Jesus." Evan took off his toque and scratched his unwashed hair. "What kinda shit do you think Scott's up to? Is he hunting and black marketing meat? What's he taking for payment? That guy does nothin' for free."

"Fuck if I know." Isaiah's shoulders slumped as he headed back into the light where a lineup of restless people was forming.

TWENTY-FIVE

Darkness seeped into the house as the sun set. Nicole pinched the tiny copper wheel to turn up the wick of the glass lamp and lit it with a black lighter. The corner of the kitchen was revealed as the flame caught. She picked up the stack of colouring books and moved them to a lower shelf, in case they became a fire hazard. The children had coloured everything in them but they still enjoyed looking at them from time to time. Nicole was conscious that sometime soon, even this light source would disappear with their supply of kerosene.

Nangohns and Maiingan sat on the floor in front of Dan. Their grandfather relaxed back into the soft chair. Nicole stepped to the couch and sat down between Evan and Patricia. It was story time.

Dan leaned forward and cleared his throat. He looked deep into the children's eyes. Maiingan flashed a smile missing baby teeth in the bottom row. They loved hearing stories — especially from their grandfather.

"Do youse kids know the one about Nanabush and the geese?" he asked. The lamplight glimmered in his brown eyes. The children shook their heads. The adults on the other side of the room cradled mugs of hot tea that had been made from boiled snow on the stove in the basement. Evan tried to relax after a long day of walking through heavy snow checking on elders and carrying loads of firewood indoors. The muscles in his back were tense.

"Well, it was early in the fall a long time ago," Dan continued. "Nanabush was getting really hungry. He knew winter was coming and that he had to get ready. He didn't have much food saved up yet. You know how me and your daddy go hunting a lot before the snow comes?"

They both nodded.

"Well, Nanabush was behind. He shoulda been hunting for weeks. But he was getting lazy. He was too busy swimming and eating the berries that come late in the summer. But then those ran out. And he decided it was finally time to go looking for food. So he walked down to the lake to try and find some geese.

"He walked for a really long time and didn't see any. 'Did they already fly south for the winter?' he asked himself. 'If they did, I'm in real trouble.' He knew that the snow was still a couple weeks away. But sometimes the ones with wings know the seasons better than we do. For all he knew, they could already be gone.

"He kept walking up the shoreline, looking all around him and listening. Then all of a sudden he heard something in the bush up from the shore. It sounded like singing and yelling. He couldn't tell what exactly it was, so he walked up the little hill into the bush. 'Who's making all that noise?' he said.

"He came to a clearing in the bush, and he saw the geese! They were singing and dancing around. They looked really happy. Like it was a party! So Nanabush walked up to the one closest to him. 'Goose!' he said. 'Why are you all singing and dancing?'

"'We are leaving soon for the winter, Nanabush,' said the tallest goose. 'We are giving thanks and asking for a safe journey and good health along the way.'

"Nanabush looked around. He counted thirty geese in that circle in the bush! Can you count to thirty?" Dan asked his grandchildren.

"Oh, I can!" Maiingan raised his hand and rapidly fired off numbers until he reached the mark.

"Well done, my boy!" said Dan. "Now do it in your native language." The boy repeated the numbers in Anishinaabemowin, which took a little longer.

Dan picked the story back up. "So the geese were leaving for the winter. Do you know the Anishinaabe word for winter?"

Nangohns's hand shot up. "Biboon!"

"Ehn, yes, my girl. That's right! Good job." He looked above them to see Evan, Nicole, and Patricia smiling on the couch.

To conserve precious resources, the families did most things together, rotating the hosting responsibilities. The idea was to save on firewood and food by living more communally. The only unpredictable variable was Cam. Sydney and their son stayed with her parents, but Evan knew Cam often wasn't there. He would return to the duplexes where Scott ruled.

"So anyways, the geese were all dancing around and singing." Dan's gestures became more animated as the story's action built. "They were very plump, because they had to eat a lot for their journey south. They needed lots of energy to fly that far.

Nanabush started licking his lips. *Look at all these geese*, he thought. *They're enough for me to get through the winter! And they're so fat!*

"Nanabush was the trickster. So he started to think of a plan to trick them. 'My brothers and sisters,' he said. 'Let me join you in your celebration. I want to wish you well on your journey to the South, so I'd like to offer you a dance.'

"'That's very kind of you, Nanabush,' said the tallest goose. He was the leader. 'We would be honoured if you joined our celebration. Please feel free to offer us your dance.'

"'Okay,' said Nanabush. 'It goes like this. You have to close your eyes and spin around in a circle. You have to keep your wings by your side. It's like you're imagining yourself in your warm new home for the winter.'" Dan stood up and demonstrated the move for the children. They giggled as he spun around with his eyes closed and a silly grin on his face.

"So the geese said okay, and they started to dance like Nanabush showed them. He looked around, and they all were spinning in circles with their eyes closed. He walked up to the big one closest to him that he'd been talking to. He kept real quiet and slowly moved his hands down to the goose's neck."

He mimicked the motion, leaning forward and peering into the kids' eyes. They sat totally still.

"Then he wrung his neck!" He thrust his hands forward in threatening grips and startled them. "Then he sneaked over to the next closest one and did the same thing. And then the next one, and the next one, and the next one. They were all dancing with their eyes closed and singing, so they didn't hear him. At the end of his evil trick, there were thirty geese lying there dead. 'Now I won't go hungry this winter!' Nanabush said to himself."

Despite their grandfather's jovial tone, Nangohns's and Maiingan's eyes slid over to their parents, who continued to sip their tea, unconcerned.

"So Nanabush took all the dead geese out of the bush and

piled them up by the shoreline," Dan went on. "He stacked them neatly. It was a long day, and he was really hungry, so he started a fire to cook one of the geese. 'I am so hungry and I am so tired,' he said. 'But I'm happy with my new bounty for the winter. I have all this food to myself!'

"But he was so tired, and he knew it would take some time to cook the first fat goose that he just stuck in the fire. So he decided he would take a little nap. To make sure he woke up in time before the goose got burnt, he asked his diiyosh — his bum — to wake him up."

"His bum!?" squealed Nangohns.

"Yes, his bum!"

Both children kicked back in laughter.

"Nanabush turned and looked at his diiyosh and he said, 'Okay, diiyosh, you better wake me up. I don't want to burn that goose. I'm just going to have a quick sleep. You make sure it turns out okay. Keep an eye out too. Make sure no one takes all our food.' So then Nanabush went to sleep. He slept for a really long time. Longer than he wanted to. Then all of a sudden he woke up. He was startled because the sun was starting to set and his diiyosh hadn't woken him up.

"Nanabush looked right at the fire. It had become really big! He saw the goose's long legs sticking out of the fire on the rocks at the edge of the firepit. He went to grab them to pull out the goose, but the legs were all that was left! The goose was in there for so long that it totally burned up. He looked at the legs in each of his hands and got really mad. Then he remembered the rest of the geese! He turned around quickly and saw that the whole pile was gone! Something came and took them all while he was asleep.

"'Diiyosh!' he yelled. 'You were supposed to keep an eye out! Now our supper is burnt and our food for the whole winter is gone!' Nanabush was so mad that he wanted to punish his diiyosh for not doing the job he asked it to do. 'I know!' he said. 'I'm going to put you in the fire as punishment for not following my orders. You'll know from now on to listen to me!' So Nanabush sat down on the edge of the firepit and put his diiyosh in the fire."

"He put his bum in the fire?!" said Maiingan. "Why would he want to hurt himself?"

Dan tilted his head sideways and continued. "It did start to hurt! It only took a few seconds, and Nanabush's diiyosh was totally on fire. 'Owwwwww!' he screamed. He jumped up really fast and started running around in circles." He sprung from his chair and shuffled quickly around the kids' spot on the floor, circling them while holding his butt. High-pitched laughter soared through the room.

"He was panicking!" Dan raised his voice, standing in front of them. "His diiyosh was on fire, and he needed to put it out! But he was too far from the water just to jump in, so he ran and jumped bum-first onto the rocks and slid down. He kept sliding down the rocks on his diiyosh until the fire was out. He kept going until all the burnt skin came off his diiyosh."

He paused and sat back down. "So you know all those green things you see on rocks in the summertime? Some are like little plants. Some just look like skin on the rock."

The children both nodded.

"That's from Nanabush's burnt bum. When he slid down the rocks, it left all that behind. Some people call that green stuff 'moss' and 'lichen.'"

Evan spoke up behind them. "Neat, eh? Can you think of any other important lessons in that story?"

"I know! I know!" said Maiingan, shooting up his hand.

"What's that?"

"Don't be greedy!"

"Don't be greedy!" Nangohns echoed.

"That's right," Evan said. "And always be ready for winter."

TWENTY-SIX

The volunteers gathered again at the shop to prepare for another food handout. The morning was again crisp and frigid, exacerbating the gnawing hunger in the guts of the people who woke up at sunrise to beat the rush before the usual long line formed.

"We gotta keep an eye on a few of them," said Tyler, alluding to some people who had become unruly the week before and some who were suspected of hoarding supplies from others, especially the elderly. They'd speculated whether Scott was intimidating people into handing over food or trading it for the few drops of contraband booze that remained.

"So what are we eating this week?" asked Evan.

Terry leaned back in his chair and rubbed his stringy beard. He tilted his chair forward to look at a sheet of scrawled notes, the makeshift inventory of the food supplies. "Uhhh . . . chilli."

"Chilli it is," said Tyler. He turned to Evan and gave him a friendly slap in the gut. "Let's go."

They marched into the back of the machine shop. Except for Isaiah tending the fire in the furnace, the room was dark. Their breath still plumed in the cold, and the air was heavy with the smell of machine grease. They shone small plastic flashlights onto the stacks of boxes piled to the right and the beams danced across the scattered stacks of supplies that had dwindled considerably. Evan's flashlight located the boxes at the far end of the wall labelled *Chilli*, and they began the task of hauling them back to the front room and stacking them in front of Terry, who was still peering at the inventory sheet in the faint morning light.

The place gradually warmed up with Isaiah's tending. After next week's ration day, they'd have to get more wood. They estimated they'd have about eight more ration days before the snow melted and people could turn their attention to planting gardens and foraging the wild spring plants. The cache would not last forever, and they had to produce the next season's food.

"There's only one box left," said Tyler.

"Just one?" asked Evan, a couple of steps behind him.

"Yeah, I can't see any more lying around."

"Shit, me neither," he said. "Let's go tell Terry."

Terry leaned forward with his elbows on his knees and ran his fingers through his hair before he let out a slow "Goddamn." There were only a little over two hundred cans of chilli left and this didn't match his inventory. He was sure there should be more but he didn't know where they could have gone.

"There's not gonna be enough," Terry conceded. "Go back and get some boxes of that canned ham."

"They're gonna be upset," said Isaiah, coming in from the back. "They just got that last week. No one likes leftovers."

Terry failed to notice the sarcasm. "I don't give a shit. It's a free fuckin' handout!"

"Whoa whoa whoa, chill! I was just kidding."

"Funny guy. Go get the corn and beans then."

Terry arranged the tables in a row in front of the supplies, facing the door. It opened, letting in a burst of cold air ahead of Jeff Whitesky and Walter and Dave Meegis.

People would be arriving soon. They had been coming earlier every week, as worry over depleting supplies simmered through many homes. For many of the families that didn't hunt or fish, months of eating canned food was wearing on them. Their diet was a rotation of cans of ham, tuna, sausages, corn, peas, beans, various soups, and other non-perishables. They complained bitterly but they still felt entitled to the food, and took the band's preparedness for granted. Who knew how they would cope when the stores ran out.

Amanda Jones and Debbie McCloud walked through the door. "Morning, boys," Amanda said. "What's on the menu today?"

Holding up his scribbled list, Walter peered over his glasses at them. "Chilli, ham, beans, and corn."

"Yum!" said Debbie, sarcastically. She rubbed her belly. She was thinner now like most others.

"Thanks for coming," said Terry, from the corner. He was still nominally the chief, but the strongest members of the council — especially Walter — had taken over a lot of the decision-making. Terry couldn't bear to make the tough choices that might alienate some of the townspeople. And these days, all their choices were tough ones.

They organized the dole line mostly in silence. Occasionally, someone would crack a cheap joke or tease another. The people in that room had accepted that life as they had become accustomed to in the last two decades would not return.

The building finally warmed up. Debbie untied her heavy black boots so she could take off her snow pants. Amanda removed her red parka and draped it over one of the chairs. The door cracked open and a sharp ray of sunshine shot across the floor. A hooded head and scarfed face poked through the small opening. "Is it food day?" Evan recognized Katie Birch, who had moved into her mother Vera's place with her three kids.

"Ehn biindigen," Walter said from his seat, waving her in.

Katie walked in and closed the door behind her. She pulled down her scarf and pushed back the hood of her jacket. She pulled three canvas bags out of her pockets. She smiled as she approached the table, revealing stained teeth. Toothpaste was another of the household items gone from people's lives.

"What you need today, sweetie?" asked Debbie. "You still at your mom's place?"

"Yep," Katie replied. "Me and the kids are still there. Just the five of us still. My brother's still at my place, but I haven't seen him in a few days. I have a feeling he might come to my mom's too, though. It's cold there, and Scott's cheap with the firewood. Keeps it all to himself."

Terry looked down at his sheet. "Youse guys got any of that moose meat left?"

"Yep, we still got some. It probably won't last much longer though."

"Hmmmmm."

"Okay, let's see your bags then," said Amanda. "We're running out of chilli. Hope you don't mind ham in a can."

"Whatever you got," Katie replied. "I'm just happy youse guys are doing this. We'd be pretty hungry by now if you didn't."

Tyler and Evan filled her bags with four cans of chilli, ten cans of the ham, ten cans of beans, and eight cans of corn.

Homes with small children got priority with the protein-rich food, and the staff and council decided who needed what at their own discretion. They were growing suspicious of some people they believed were abusing the handouts.

Isaiah and Evan brought the bags back to Katie, who offered a simple miigwech and a smile before going back out the door and loading them on her plastic sled to pull home.

The morning proceeded mostly in quiet routine. Twenty cans of canned ham went to some. Fifteen went to others. They tried to spread out the chilli sparingly and fairly. Brandon Jones said he needed more cans of meat because his brother Matt's family had just moved in with them. Jeff reminded him that they'd eventually have to get out and hunt. Brandon didn't appreciate what he felt was scolding and told him to fuck off as he left.

By midday, a lineup had formed that snaked out the door and around the building. People held large backpacks, empty hockey bags, and plastic sleds at their sides, anticipating heavy hauls. Many faces had lost colour and some bore even the yellow stain of malnutrition.

Inside, the crew worked as quickly as possible to fill bags and answer questions. None had expected this sudden rush to the handout. There were lineups in previous weeks, but they hadn't formed this quickly. It made them all uneasy. *What's behind this?* thought Evan. What kind of rumours were going around that they hadn't heard?

People in the line grew restless. With the door propped open as people tried to squeeze in, the team could hear shouting outside. Walter told Evan, Isaiah, and Tyler to go out and investigate.

Outside the shouts were crisp, cutting accusations and threats. "Fuck you, you're the one who butted in front of me!" yelled one man. Evan recognized his cousin Jason. "Fuck that, asshole, step back!" said another man. He saw the tussle brewing about halfway down the line. As they approached, they could see that it was Tyler's brother fighting with Jason.

"Whoa whoa whoa!" Tyler shouted. "Break it up!" He stepped between their punches, taking a couple errant blows to the face in the process. Their heavy jackets and sweaters slowed their swings, but the men were bloody, with split lips and crunched noses. Others stepped in to pull them apart but soon got caught up in the violence and began scrapping with each other. Pent-up tension exploded along the line and it quickly descended into an all-out brawl.

Men and women swore and yelled. Adrenaline surged through Evan as he saw blood dripping from his cousin's ashen face. They didn't get along, but Jason was still family. He ploughed in, pulling at arms, punching at any face he could see until he found himself toe-to-toe with Tyler.

He lunged forward, wrapping his arms around Tyler's torso and driving him into the side of the shop. His cap came off and his long brown hair flew about. The slam knocked the wind out of Tyler. "What the fuck, Ev?" he grunted out as he tried to get his breath back. "Calm down! What are you doing?" He pushed at Evan's arms to free himself from the grip.

Four sharp cracks of gunfire pierced the havoc, bringing silence to the melee. Justin Scott stood at the bottom of the road leading up to the shop, holding a handgun in the air. Despite the freezing temperatures, his bald head was bare, bouncing the sunlight back up to the sky. To his right stood Brad Connor, another of the newcomers.

Scott lowered the gun to his side and walked forward, the other man a step behind him. "Settle down."

Evan and Tyler stood side by side, with dishevelled jackets and tussled hair. Scott looked at them. "Jesus Christ, what's gotten into you two? I thought you were supposed to be the reasonable ones around here?"

Evan looked down at his boots. His damn temper had gotten out of control again, which hardly ever happened before all this. "They ran out of the fruit cocktail in there," Tyler quipped. Evan snorted and wiped his warm snot on his sweater sleeve. He looked back at Scott, who just shook his head.

"Is the whole gang inside?" Scott asked Evan, who nodded. "Alright then." He looked to Connor and gestured with his head in the direction of the building. "Let's go."

Both men strolled past the queue of hungry people, who stared at them in resentment. Scott towered over everyone else in the community, even Tyler, and Connor was only a few inches shorter. Their pale faces shimmered in the daylight. Scott ignored everyone, but Connor surveyed the line cautiously. Scott threw the door open and walked inside.

Debbie, Walter, and Terry looked up to see the men stroll in ahead of the line. Walter sighed, and Terry guided his expression to neutrality. Debbie handed a bag to a young father at the front of the line and asked, "What's up, boys?"

"Oh, we just came by to see how the handouts were going today," Scott answered. He sauntered towards the table and sat down in one of the open chairs at the side. Connor stayed at the wall by the door. He scratched his thick red beard before putting his hands in the pockets of his snowmobile jacket.

"Steady as she goes," Debbie replied.

"Really?" Scott cocked his head. "Because it looked like you had a brawl outside just a couple minutes ago."

"People are hungry," Debbie shrugged. "It's cold out today too."

The people standing in the inside food line watched Scott uneasily. He looked at the line of brown faces with hollowing cheeks. The heads without toques or ball caps were shaggy and greasy. The growing desperation was palpable and none of the leadership in the room could deny it.

"If you guys want some, you're gonna have to go to the back of the line," Debbie said as she handed another full canvas bag back to a young woman. "We gotta keep this going."

Scott cleared his throat and fixed his eyes on Terry and Walter, who were trying to focus on the lists of people and supplies in front of them. "I think we're good for today, thanks," he declared, as if to make some kind of point. "We snared a few pretty big rabbits the other day. That's probably more than you can say for anyone else here."

Terry's eyes cut sharply to Scott. Scott stood up and stepped closer to them. The young woman waiting for her food shuffled backwards. He put both hands on the table and leaned in. His deep-set blue eyes moved from Terry to Walter to Debbie and back.

"I know you're running out," he whispered. "And if you think you can just brush off shit like what just happened outside, you're delusional." He leaned in closer. "They're gonna go crazy. They're gonna get violent. And when the last can goes from that room in the back there, they're gonna come for you. Unless they get their shit together, you're gonna have a serious crisis on your hands."

Terry's fists clenched on the surface of the table. The hot furnace air felt dry in Evan's throat. Scott brought his whisper down even lower, but not too low, so the first few people near the table could hear his foreboding message. "You're gonna have to think about feeding your people. And you're running out of options. But I know where we can find something else to eat, and I think you know what I mean."

Scott stood up and smiled, his mouth cavernous and dark behind his big teeth "Chi-miigwech for your time, Chief," he said, changing his tone. "I look forward to discussing this matter with you again."

He turned around and stepped out the door, with Connor following closely behind.

TWENTY-SEVEN

Evan struck the red match head against the gritty side of the box. A tiny orange flame crackled to life, giving off a small puff of grey smoke. The sulphur lingered for a moment, stinging his nostrils. Pinching the match between his calloused, dirt-stained thumb and forefinger, he turned the match to let the flame crawl along the small wooden stick.

It began as an orange teardrop and stretched as it crawled along the stick. As it elongated, the flame peaked at either end, like a smile. The cold air above it shimmered from the small pocket of heat. The fire crawled away from the match head, leaving curved, charred remains that almost looked like a burnt tadpole. The flame mesmerized Evan and he didn't realize he was under its spell until he felt it burn his fingers. He shook the flame out and threw the match on the ground before lighting another.

He lit the second one and, after letting it burn for a second, placed it in an opening in the meticulously piled wood in front of him. The burning spruce and pine smelled familiar and comforting. As the orange flames emerged from the heart of the pile, a grey plume rippled upwards through the opening in the green canvas tarp above him, blending with the overcast sky that peeked through.

Evan sunk back to sitting on the old brown sleeping bag and savoured the peace as the fire crackled to life in front of him. The ground around him was clear of snow: he had shovelled out as much as he could on his last trip here, and the fire he'd lit during that visit had warmed the interior enough to melt away the remnants.

This was Evan's secret project: a shelter in the bush that he had begun the day after the food brawl. A backup, in case he and his family needed refuge from whatever turmoil might eventually consume his community. He had begun by chopping the long, straight narrow spruce trees that would be the pillars and stripping their bark. A few days later, he had sledded out the three thick canvases, one at a time. Each trip took a full morning. He came back a few days after that to dig out a firepit and drape the tarps over the tipi frame. Here he was, weeks later, beginning to outfit the safe haven.

A pile of neatly folded wool blankets lay on the ground on the far side of the structure. Two boxes of assorted canned goods were stacked on the right. He planned to wrap the boxes with some of the blankets to insulate them from the freezing temperatures that would last another couple of months. He would have to rebuild the structure in the spring to let the poles cure properly, but for now, this experiment seemed to be working.

Evan looked over the dancing flames at the load he had just dragged over the snow. He slid his right hand into the pocket of his parka and pulled out a small purple drawstring cloth bag that had once held a stubby heavy bottle of whiskey. Its contents rattled as he bounced the satchel lightly in his cracked palm.

The bag held a simple can opener and ten small boxes of matches; an emergency supply to open the food and start a fire should he and his family have to escape to this tent in the bush. He surveyed the ground around him for a place to bury the bag. He felt about under the decomposing leaves that had been crushed into the yellow grass by the snow. The vegetation felt damp, and below the ground was frozen. He slammed the heel of his boot into the earth and a shock reverberated through his foot. The ground was still too frozen to dig.

But the fire had warmed the inside of the tent. Evan stood up to take off his heavy parka. The tipi stood almost three times his height, and he easily stepped around the fire to throw the bag overtop the boxes and blankets. As he leaned over to pick up one of the blankets, a drop of sweat fell from his long black bangs. He wiped the perspiration from his brow with the tattered sleeve of his black hoodie. *How long was I sitting in front of the fire?* he thought.

He pulled the top blanket off the pile and shook it open. It reeked of mustiness, like the corner of the basement from which he'd grabbed it. It was one of a few old blankets put aside for emergency situations. He couldn't remember when he had stashed this one away but it clearly hadn't been used in a very long time.

Evan shook it out one more time and let it fall gently on the ground. He turned back to the pile and picked up an orange blanket the same size and make as the first. He flapped it open, making the flames dance and grow. He laid it over the grey one and sat down on the insulated ground.

Sitting cross-legged, he stared into the fire, then leaned on one elbow so he could stretch out his legs. His people didn't make tipis. They weren't characteristic of the Anishinaabeg. But he learned how to build one from a how-to guide in a hunting magazine of all places. He and Isaiah experimented with different sizes on random excursions into the bush over the years. Right now, it was the easiest, most reliable thing he could build in the middle of the winter in a power crisis.

The warmth relaxed him, and the stillness inside the tipi soothed him. He felt the stiffness in his upper back ease. The peaceful winter day outside left the tarps undisturbed on the poles. Evan rested his head on the inside of his arm, closed his eyes, and fell asleep.

A blizzard howled as he opened the high garage door, the whiteout obscuring his line of sight. He looked up to see a crimson sun pulsing through the winter storm, washing the snow around him in a bright red glow like the flashing lights of an ambulance. It seemed to flash in sync with the beat of his heart, which sped up as he stepped into the building to escape the storm. He pulled back the hood of his parka and his eyes struggled to adjust to the darkness. The pulsating flares from the sun outside did nothing to illuminate the interior of the morgue.

He couldn't make out the neatly arranged lines of bodies. His hands trembled under his thick snowmobile mitts. He panicked and bit on the end of the right mitt to pull his hand out and thrust it into his pocket to grab his flashlight. His hands shook as he cradled the light close to his chest and struggled to find the switch. The red light from the outside intensified and his breath grew shorter. His chest was tight and he struggled for air. To his relief, he located the button and the blueish light shot upward and back down to the floor as he got his panicked hands under control.

All that remained were the old, tattered blankets that had wrapped the bodies. It looked like they had decomposed into nothing.

His heartbeat echoed loudly in his ears. A fierce trembling overcame his whole body and his pupils dilated. A deep, guttural growl boomed behind him and drowned out the howl of the wind. Whatever stood in the snow just outside the garage door wheezed as it drew in a breath, and let out a harsh, threatening snarl at a pitch just higher than a bear's. Evan stiffened, momentarily paralyzed, before he summoned the courage to turn and face it.

A feral odor, like a rotting heap of moose innards, wafted briskly into the garage. A tall, gaunt silhouette stood in the doorway, outlined by the scarlet blizzard behind it. The smell made him gag. The creature hunched forward. The hair on its broad shoulders and long arms blurred the lines of its figure. Its legs appeared disfigured, almost backwards. But its large, round head scared him the most. It breathed out another savage rumble.

Evan slowly raised the flashlight, illuminating the figure's pale, heaving emaciated torso under sparse brown body hair. He brought the beam up to its face. It was disfigured yet oddly familiar. Scott. His cheeks and lips were pulled tight against his skull. He breathed heavily through his mouth, with long incisors jutting upward and downward from rows of brown teeth. His eyes were blacked out. If it weren't for the large, bald scalp and the long, pointy noise, this monster would have been largely unrecognizable.

The beast Scott had become lunged forward.

TWENTY-EIGHT

The water bubbled in the big black pot on top of the wood stove in the basement. Wearing thick oven mitts, Nicole grabbed the handles and turned to walk it carefully back up the stairs. The morning sunshine outside was bright enough to light the basement so she didn't need to juggle a flashlight as well.

Her hands ached and her arms trembled by the time she made it upstairs. She trudged across the kitchen floor and grimaced as she hoisted the pot of hot water onto the useless electric stove. She turned to the sink to arrange the clothes she was about to wash. Underwear, socks, and T-shirts always got priority, with jeans and sweaters going through only if they began to stink. She scooped a small amount of powdered detergent out of the bottom of the box and sprinkled the grains sparingly over the laundry.

Nicole grabbed the pot of water and poured it into the wash basin. As it splashed onto the clothes and steam swelled into her face, she turned her head to the living room behind her. "How you guys doing in there?"

"Good," Nangohns replied. "We're building a new house for Nookomis and Mishomis!"

Nicole put the empty pot back on the stove top and picked up the wooden spoon beside the sink to mix the detergent into the clothes. "A new house! I'm gonna have to come and see that!"

She looked into the living room, where she saw her children sitting on the carpet, playing with toy blocks. Nangohns's pink sweatshirt was fading and the holes in the knees of Maiingan's small jeans were growing daily. Both kids would outgrow these clothes soon anyway, and somehow they'd have to find some bigger ones soon. They both looked up at her, smiling.

"Why do Nookomis and Mishomis need a new house?" Nicole asked. "Theirs is still in good shape,"

"This one's their summer house," replied Maiingan.

"Summer house!" echoed the girl.

"Oh, I see. Why do they need a summer house?" Nicole untied her bun and regathered it more tightly and neatly.

"Just in case," Maiingan said and turned his eyes back down to the interlocking plastic.

"Just in case, eh," she muttered. "Well, I gotta go outside just for a minute."

"Okay, Mommy," Nangohns answered.

Nicole went back to the kitchen to get the pot and came back through the living room to put on her winter boots. She didn't bother grabbing her jacket from the coat rack. She opened the door, went quickly out into the chill, and dipped the pot into the high snow. She packed the snow into the pot and brought it back into the house.

By anyone's guess, it was mid-March. Terry Meegis was probably the only one who still knew the exact date. Nicole preferred to wait out the winter rather than lament the days since the power went out or generate any false optimism about how close it was to spring.

But the more tolerable temperatures and heavier snow indicated that winter had peaked. At least a month and a half of snow and cold remained, but the days were longer and the twilight hung long over the horizon in the luminous blue that foretold spring. Soon there would be no more snowmelt for drinking, cooking, and washing water and they would have to figure something else out. There would be no return to running water.

Back in the basement, Nicole dumped the snow into the large plastic basin a few metres from the wood stove. A collection of basins, buckets, and bins held melted snow water. On the other side, a smaller number of large pots contained water that had already been boiled for consumption. It was an efficient rotation and it hadn't taken too long for them to adjust. After all, it was how Dan and Patricia's generation had grown up.

Nicole heard a knock. She put the pot on the floor and walked upstairs to see Tyler standing at the door. Two braids hung behind his ears and his grey toque was pulled down over his eyebrows. He feigned a weak smile when he saw her. Without going all the way to the door, she waved him in.

Tyler stepped inside and closed the door. He looked at the kids on the floor and smiled. "Boozhoo binoojiinyag!" he declared warmly. "Hey, kids! Whatcha doing?"

"Making houses!" Nangohns replied.

"Oh, ever good houses. We'll need to give youse guys a job next summer!"

Tyler turned to Nicole.

"What's up?" she asked.

"Is Ev around?"

"No, he went out into the bush to check some snares."

"When do you think he'll be back?"

"I dunno. Probably soon. He left pretty early this morning. What's going on?"

He sighed, and his broad shoulders drooped. "Auntie Aileen died."

Nicole covered her mouth. Tears welled in her brown eyes.

TWENTY-NINE

Evan ran the back of his moose-hide glove across his face. The rabbit-fur trim collected his tears. He struggled not to sob as he and Tyler pulled Aileen's body across the heavy snow. His chest felt tight, his arms heavy, and his legs burned as he lifted each snowshoe forward.

He had arrived home from his trip into the bush the day before to find Tyler walking down the steps. Aileen's niece Amanda had gone to check on her and found her dead, bundled in her bed at home.

Evan had felt numb at first and he hadn't cried over Aileen's death until later at night. She had been his surrogate grand-mother, his go-to elder whenever he had questions about the old ways, and he had loved her. He hoped she had enjoyed his visits, for they had always been special to him. He had known she would go eventually, but he had hoped that it would not be this soon.

The smell of sage smudge lingered in his nose, and the travelling song her family had sung for her rang in his ears. Before Evan and Tyler had shown up, her children and grandchildren had debated over where she should go. Tradition called for four days of grieving and celebration before giving a body back to the earth, but the ground was still too hard for burial. So her family had spent the night singing songs and making initial preparations for her journey to the spirit world, outfitting her with the traditional medicines and tools she needed to cross over safely.

Their snowshoes flapped against their boots. Tyler cleared his throat. "Uh, so how are we supposed to put her in there?" he asked nervously. Neither wanted to look back at the elder's body wrapped in dark grey blankets on a bed of cedar boughs.

"I think we're just supposed to smudge around her," Evan answered, patting his front left pocket to feel for the sweetgrass Amanda had handed him. "Then we have to put down tobacco and ask for her to be safe there."

"Okay. Are we supposed to do a song or anything else?"

"No, Amanda said they'd come down later to do another song."

"Alright," Tyler said in obvious relief. These protocols were new to him too.

They walked up over the hill that used to be the driveway to the office. The road lay at least a metre and a half beneath the snow, but it was easier to walk across now that it was late winter. The powder had compacted and they sank less each day. The walls of the band office came into view, and Evan took a deep breath.

The air was damp. The sled glided along with a muffled

whoosh. Evan and Tyler guided it carefully towards the building that once bustled with life but now only housed the dead. Their regular trips here throughout the winter had made trails and a clearing in the snow in front of the garage door that clanked and rattled as Tyler pulled the chains from the inside.

Their sorrow kept them silent. Evan pulled the sled slowly onto the cold concrete floor. He dropped the yellow rope and finally turned to look at the elder's body. The rolled blankets fit snugly around Aileen's small frame. He pictured her resting peacefully on her bed of cedar.

"I hate to say this," Tyler said, breaking the silence. "But I think we're gonna have to do some rearranging in here."

Evan looked back to the three rows of bodies that stretched wall to wall, and from the back nearly all the way to the door. "Goddamn, I think you're right."

The death toll had reached twenty-two. Twenty-three, if you counted Mark Phillips, the man Justin Scott had killed at the beginning of winter. But his body was not here. It still lay on the outskirts of the reserve, frozen and buried in snow where it had been left in the moments after he was shot. There was still some room at the front, but it was small and cramped by the door, and both men wanted to give Aileen the dignity of sufficient space.

"Alright, let's go see how we can do this." Evan stepped through the bodies to the back. It was darker the deeper they went into the garage, and the bodies that lay towards the far wall were no more than silhouettes in the dim light.

The friends remembered exactly which person lay where, the circumstances around their death, and the day they brought them to this unfair and uncertain industrial tomb. Both thought of the spring to come, of the necessity of digging twenty-three plots by hand, and burying each person in the rez cemetery. It would be a daunting, traumatic task.

Evan sighed. "Well, let's move them all a bit closer together to make more room at the front."

"Yeah, that's probably the best way to do it," Tyler agreed. "If we just move them all a little bit to the side, that'll open up some room on the ends."

Evan nodded. Tyler continued, "And I hate to say this too, but there'll probably be at least a couple more people who won't make it out of this winter alive."

Evan didn't want to think about this so instead he said, "Help me over on this end," and walked carefully to the far corner, where they positioned the winter's first fatalities. He stopped at Jenna Jones's feet to face Tyler, who stood at her head. Tyler grimaced and shrugged. They squatted and Evan patted the sides of the young woman's stiff, frozen legs to find a good grip. His gloves and the few blankets around her buffered his hands from her dead limbs. *This is only her body*, he thought. *Her spirit is gone. We will return her to Mother Earth as soon as we can.* He cupped his hands under her Achilles tendons and nodded to Tyler, who shoved his hands under her shoulders. They heaved her frozen frame off the floor. It seemed lighter than when they had put her here.

Evan told himself it was like lifting a few sheets of drywall: long, heavy, and unbending. He tried to chase the memories of the night of her death from his mind. He couldn't. He felt her petite heels — the flesh of her feet now hard as stones — on the outsides of his palms, and remembered her face as he stared down into the dark cloth that wrapped her legs.

Jenna had been beautiful. Her high cheekbones accentuated the natural tan of her face and her almond-shaped eyes were nearly black. She had exuded a confident intelligence. As they set her down lightly just a foot from where she had originally lain, Evan wondered who she would have become.

"Next one?" Tyler asked. Her cousin Tara was next. They

picked her up, stiff and heavy as ice, and moved her the same distance, turning quickly to the next one. The lingering misery of the community's tragedies was suffocating.

They moved down the line methodically, trying not to acknowledge or remember the people they rearranged and the subsequent dead that were still to come. They finished squeezing together the corpses in the first row, leaving space on the end for another.

Then they hoisted the corpse closest to them and moved it into the cleared spot at the end of the first row. The young men went through the three rows, squeezing the rest of the bodies tightly together. They stood back to look at their work before moving Aileen into place.

"Wait a second," Evan said. He did a quick count. "Weren't there twenty-one here before?"

Tyler counted. ". . . nineteen, twenty. Yeah, there's twenty there."

"Yeah, remember? Johnny Meegis was the twenty-first."

"Fuck, I don't remember."

"Someone's missing."

Tyler stepped back and counted again. He took off his cap and pulled on a braid. "So what do you think?"

Evan lowered his head and took a deep breath. "I think it was Scott."

"Huh? What do you mean?"

"Scott took a body."

"Come on, man. That's crazy. What for?"

Evan paused. There was a heavy stillness in the big room. "To eat."

Tyler stared at him. He opened his mouth to speak but couldn't, and he left it agape. He finally whispered, "How are we gonna prove that?"

Evan turned to his friend. "We're gonna have to go search his house."

"What? If we show up at his place, that crazy fucker is gonna shoot us."

"That's what he meant in the food lineup when he said we were going to need him. I think he knows we have stories and stuff that say we can't do that, so he has to start it. Shit." He didn't want to think about the dream he had at the tipi.

"What?"

"Let's make sure Auntie Aileen is in place here first. Then let's go find whoever we can and go over there."

Evan stepped over to Aileen's body and waited for Tyler to follow. His mind swirled as they fitted her into place at the end of the row. She blended in, already anonymous. It didn't feel right to either of them to just leave her there.

Where's her spirit? Evan thought. *Is she on her way to the spirit world? Is she stuck here? She needs to be on her journey. This isn't right.* His throat tightened and his eyes watered.

He shook off grief, and anger returned. "Let's go see Scott," he said.

"Shouldn't we go talk to Walter or someone?" asked Tyler.

"No, they won't listen to us. They'll just call another damn meeting and do nothing. This is up to us."

THIRTY

The smell of wood burning reached them as they approached the row of duplexes. The snow swelled through their snowshoes with each step. Evan was focused on the patterns his snowshoes made. Anything not to think about what lay ahead.

"Whatever you do," he said to Isaiah and Tyler, who had come with him, "keep your gun on your shoulder. Don't walk in pointing it at him. He's a shoot-first kinda guy."

"He's a fuckin' psycho," said Isaiah. "We don't know how fast he can draw a gun."

"As long as there isn't one in his hands, we'll be one step ahead."

"Goddamn it," Isaiah sighed and turned his head away. Tyler glanced at Evan, whose gaze went cold.

Evan cocked his head toward the duplex that Scott and his cronies occupied. "See that smoke? It looks like there's a fire out back."

"Shit, yeah. They must be working on something back there," said Isaiah.

"Alright, well let's just go around and make like we just wanna talk," said Evan.

"Isn't that what we want to do?" asked Isaiah. His voice cracked at the end of his question.

"Yeah . . . it is."

The plan was to confront Scott about the missing body. When they had found Isaiah at his house to tell him, he hadn't needed much convincing and had agreed with Evan. So Tyler had come along reluctantly. Over the course of this terrible winter, they had become an unbreakable alliance.

Anxiety hummed in Evan's ears as he walked towards the house. Isaiah followed, watching for an ambush. In the rear, Tyler scanned the windows of the building for any sign of the people who lived there. There was no activity.

They walked around the corner of the building and the smell of smoke grew stronger. Their hearts beat faster as they neared the back. They didn't feel the freezing temperatures stinging their bare hands, cracked and calloused after the long winter.

Evan heard the fire crackle as he rounded the duplex and entered the backyard, which was sheltered by green pine and spruce trees. Three snowmobiles were parked along the back wall of the building. Scott, Brad Connor, and Alex Richer stood around a large firepit made from an old oil drum. A large black pot rested on top of the rusty makeshift grill. Scott's back was to them but Connor stiffened and Richer raised an eyebrow as he saw the three men approach. Scott continued to stare into the fire without turning around.

"Is that my buddy Evan?" he said, almost asking the flames themselves.

"How ya doin', Justin?" Evan responded, knowing any hesitation would reveal nervousness. He called him by his first name in an attempt to play a deceptive friendly hand. Scott wore only a grey hooded sweatshirt and faded jeans. Evan couldn't see a gun on or near him. To the left, Richer also appeared unarmed in a blue plaid jack shirt. To the right of Scott, Connor stood expressionless. Evan didn't notice a gun on him either, but both men could have them concealed under their bulky jackets.

"I'm good, thanks, friend," Scott replied, slowly turning around. His hands were tucked in the pouch of his hoodie. Scott studied the three of them with a smirk. He noticed the guns over their shoulders. "You boys out huntin' or something?"

Evan smiled faintly and shrugged. "We haven't gotten anything. We must be gettin' rusty!"

"Good thing we showed up! You guys woulda been wasting away up here by now. Eh boys?" Scott cocked his head back to the men behind him, who said nothing. "White man always saves the day!" He erupted in boisterous laughter, keeping his eyes trained on the three Anishinaabe men in front of him. Without missing a beat, he abruptly stopped laughing and spoke again, this time calmly and seriously. "Alright, enough bullshit. What do you want?"

"We gotta ask you about something."

"Go on."

"Were you down at the garage lately?" Evan kept his voice steady and low.

"What garage?"

"The one down by the band office. On the other side of the building where you used to stay."

"Oh, the morgue?"

The word stung. Evan's rifle felt heavy on his shoulder. He noticed he was gritting his teeth. He was starting to lose his cool, and he knew it.

"What the hell would I want down there?" Scott shot back without taking his hands out of the front pocket of his sweatshirt. Isaiah kept his eyes on Scott's concealed fists.

"That day you were at the handout. You said something about knowing what to eat when the food runs out. Is that what you meant?"

"Oh, come on now, Ev. Why would I say something like that?"

"I heard you."

"I was probably just joking. I know how you people have all kinds of ceremonies and voodoo and shit about your dead."

Evan felt the blood rush into his face. "What's in that pot?"

Scott kept his boots planted in the snow and lowered his voice. "That? That's just a little experiment. Don't worry about it."

"It looks like you're boiling something."

Tyler breathed in, trying to smell what was in the pot but all he could sense was the woodsmoke.

Scott lowered his chin and his eyes hardened. Evan's gut fluttered.

"Do you boys remember when I came here?" said Scott.

The pair behind him squared up to face them as Scott continued. "I came here by myself. I survived for days out in the bush after everything in the city went to shit. And it was easy for me. I coulda been out there for weeks, no problem. When I got here, you people barely had your shit together. There was no plan. People were going hungry already. And your solution? Give them handouts. Now those are running out, and there'll be goddamn chaos here soon. If some of these freeloaders even survive this winter." Scott's voice rose and his eyes grew wide. "Most of them don't even know how to trap! When I took some of those kids out there, they didn't know what the fuck they were doing. If that's your future, then . . . huh." He shook his head.

Evan exhaled forcefully and let his own shoulders settle, as if he were about to squeeze a trigger with a moose in sight. "We were okay without you. And we'll be okay without you. We been up here longer than you been."

Scott squinted. "Is that a threat, Ev?"

"We don't need you, Scott."

"Bullshit."

"We know this land."

"I doubt that. Maybe you guys do. Not the rest of the dead-beats here."

"It's in all of them. They know it."

"Don't get all Indian on me now."

Evan softened his tone and bared his palms in Scott's direction. "Why did you come here, anyway?"

"Doesn't matter. I'm here now."

"What are you running from?"

"Your boys saw what was happening down there."

"Why'd you think it'd be better here?"

The door at the back porch clicked and creaked open, and Cam emerged from inside. As he closed the door behind him and came into plain sight, Evan noticed his little brother's bare arms and the front of his overalls covered in blood. Cam's gaze was locked on the firepit. Evan felt his stomach drop. "Cam!" he blurted, his voice cracking.

Cam looked at his brother and his friends standing off against the white men. His eyes cleared as he recognized the familiar faces, almost as if he were emerging from a deep spell. He looked down at his bloody hands and began to sob.

"What in the holy fuck is going on here?" shouted Isaiah.

Evan shook off the sickening feeling in his gut and asked Scott outright, "Did you steal a body?"

Scott rolled his eyes. "Fuck sakes, man. Who cares?"

"We care. Those are our relatives!"

"It doesn't matter if I did. This is a matter of survival, boys."

Evan felt Tyler tense beside him. "You're a fuckin' murderer and a fuckin' cannibal!" Tyler shouted. He made to move towards Cam, who stood frozen, but Evan held out his arm to stop him.

"Alright, everyone, calm the fuck down." Evan fought to regain control of the situation.

"Let's just have a look at what's on the fire there, Scott." He took a step towards the pot.

Scott pulled a pistol from the sweatshirt's pouch and pointed it at Evan. "Now you just hold up there, boy," he ordered. Evan stopped walking and slowly raised his hands. Tyler and Isaiah unshouldered their guns. "You both calm the fuck down too." Scott waved the barrel at them. "You've seen me use this."

"All of you, chill out," said Evan as he raised his open palms. "Let's just take a step back . . ."

Scott fired three shots, and Evan crumpled to the ground. As Scott turned to fire on Tyler and Isaiah, his head burst open above his left eye in a spray of blood, bone, and brain. He fell forward.

Meghan Connor stood on the back porch with the rifle sight up to her eye. Cam cowered on the wooden deck beside her. Her light brown hair draped over her shoulder and the butt of the gun. Her body heaved with shock. Scott lay face down, motionless, as blood leaked from his head into the snow, spreading crimson across the white.

Evan grunted, and Tyler scrambled to help him. Isaiah fixed his gun on the other two men, who put their hands up in surrender. He looked to Meghan on the porch, still holding her rifle. She nodded, and trained her gun on her husband and his friend, who froze in place. She muttered something to Cam, who remained crouched, crying into his bloody hands.

Isaiah turned his gaze back to the other men, and he knew there was nothing left to fear. Richer and Brad Connor were defeated without Scott. They were now outnumbered and out-gunned. They would likely be banished from the territory for the part they had played, but that was the community's decision. The water in the pot continued to bubble as the fire crackled beneath it. Isaiah took a few cautious steps towards it to look inside.

THIRTY-ONE

The sun broke through the clouds, striking the snow as they dragged the sled past the abandoned Northern. Months had passed since anyone had walked this way, so Tyler and Isaiah were forging a new trail in the heavy snow. Their arms burned as they dragged the body behind them and sweat dripped from their noses. They said nothing, listening only to the sound their snowshoes made and the steady shushing of the plastic sled.

No signs of life remained at this end of the community. The portal to the South was dormant and barren. The store itself lay in ruin with the door agape and the windows smashed. Isaiah squinted to look inside but couldn't make out the empty shelves or anything else in the darkness. He turned his attention back to the path in front of him and saw the small white ridge that led to the old service road just beyond it.

Isaiah and Tyler reached the incline. Neither looked back to the body behind them. Their skin was ashen and dark bags hung under their brown eyes. Tyler wiped his brow on the arm of his jacket and tucked the straggling strands of long black hair behind his ear. Isaiah adjusted the beak of his ball cap. His ears were catching a bit of a chill. He nodded at Tyler, and they summoned the strength to lift Scott's body to the top of the ridge.

The snow was soft and would soon melt, so it was easy for them to dig it in slightly and bring it to rest. They could no longer ignore the corpse. They had grown to loathe the man in his short time in their community but they pitied him in death. No one would ever know what had driven him or what had brought him to their town. Now they felt only relief that he would be gone, a blip in the communal memory of this terrible winter.

The friends looked at each other one more time, and Tyler gave the body a heavy shove. It slid slowly down the other side of the ridge. He looked away before it stopped, and both men turned to walk towards the community, the light sled skimming behind them.

Scott's body slid over where Mark Phillips's still-frozen corpse lay under a thick blanket of snow. It came to a rest in a slight dip in the snow. It was left to freeze in the waning weeks of winter, and when the melt came, the crows and wolves would arrive for a taste of flesh.

ZIIGWAAN
SPRING

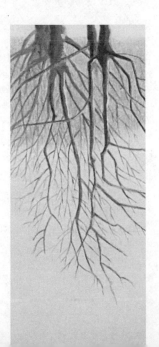

Nicole lifted her sunglasses and rested them on her head as she turned back into the house for one last pass-through. The frames rested in the weave of the braid tied tightly against her scalp. She stood in the living room and gazed at the stripped-down surroundings.

The pictures were gone from the walls. The cushions had been pulled from the couch and the chairs. Anything wooden, such as a coffee or side tables, had long been removed. The large black rectangle of a television remained on the wall but it had been two winters now since it flickered.

She walked through the living room and into the kitchen where the absent cupboard doors exposed a small stack of dishes. The essentials had been moved out weeks before. All the kitchen furniture was also gone, taken out and stored for fire fuel.

Nicole had done her best to ignore any nostalgia for this home she and Evan had created for their family. The children were still young. They would forget. But the memories in this place were strong and lasting for her. She didn't know if they would ever return, but she had stored a small collection of mementos in a corner of the basement in case they could someday come back for them.

Nicole started towards the door to the basement to go down and sort through the pile one last time, but she stopped and shook her head. She had already packed two photo albums and made bundles for both Maiingan and Nangohns to carry on their journeys to remind them of how their life once was.

So she decided not to go back downstairs and left the rest of the pictures, baby toys, electronics, and other mementos in a pile under the white wedding dress she never got to wear. She and Evan had always planned to get married eventually, and she was going to wear her mother's wedding dress. But holding that kind of event made no sense now, and they'd never be able to mark an anniversary anyway. Still, she put her faith in the belief that this was not the last time she'd be in this place.

She pulled her scratched sunglasses back down over her eyes and walked back out into the mid-morning sunshine. It gleamed on her bare brown shoulders. She shut the door behind her without locking it and stepped down the creaky stairs. Her kids and their grandparents waited for her in the driveway.

Dan Whitesky leaned against the warm blue metal of Evan's old truck with his arms crossed, his red cap pulled low to shade his eyes. Nicole's father stood beside him, dressed similarly, but in different faded colours. They tied their long hair behind their heads with tiny strips of deer hide, concealing the ponytails. Her mother, Theresa stood in front of them, comfortable in her dirty grey T-shirt, tattered jean shorts, and sandals as the summer morning heated up. In the shade on the grass on the other side of the driveway, Patricia Whitesky and the two children threw a wobbly yellow frisbee back and forth.

Nicole approached the truck. Theresa put her arms around Nicole without saying anything. They broke the embrace, and Nicole stepped back to lift her glasses and wipe her eyes. Almost on cue, the children ran up to her, not sensing anything wrong. She smiled and laughed as they each wrapped their arms around her legs.

Maiingan looked up at her. His long brown hair fell over his shoulders now, as long as his little sister's. Seven years old, the boy was growing taller. He had grown up so much since the lights went out nearly two years before, but his youthful exuberance remained intact. "Did you get my fishing rod, Mommy?" he asked.

"Yes, my boy," she replied. His joy and enthusiasm grounded her and always reassured her about their family's road ahead. "Your tackle box too. It's all in there," she motioned with her head to the packed trailer that the adults would take turns pulling into the bush.

The structures they were leaving behind would likely stand for a few more generations. The homes were perfectly viable shelters from the cold and rain. The band office, the shop, and all the other community buildings would probably last even longer. And all the infrastructure was most likely still functional. But there was no use for any of it.

Along with half the people who had lived here, the fledgling spirit they had been trying to nourish in this place had died. There was no use staying somewhere that had become so tragic. The bad memories and the sadness had smothered the good so many people had worked so hard to sustain, even in the wake of the darkness that befell them.

And when it became clear to them that they were never supposed to last in this situation on this land in the first place, they decided to take control of their own destiny. Their ancestors were displaced from their original homeland in the South and the white people who forced them here had never intended for them to survive. The collapse of the white man's modern systems further withered the Anishinaabeg here. But they refused to wither completely, and a core of dedicated people had worked tirelessly to create their own settlement away from this town.

They also couldn't be certain there wouldn't be more visitors. None had come since the arrival of those from the South in those first scary months. But if civilized life remained in the cities and towns around them, the mass migration was likely already underway. No one wanted to deal with any more of them. Not now.

"Is my fishing rod in there too, Mommy?" asked Nangohns, now old enough to know how to cast — or at least drop — a line into the water.

"You bet, my girl."

"Can we go fishing today?"

"Probably. It won't take us that long to get there."

"Yay!" the five-year-old started jumping up and down.

Patricia put her hand on Nicole's shoulder. "Well, you ready?"

"As ready as I'm gonna be."

"Okay then, let's go."

Nicole nodded and looked back down at her son and daughter. "Okay, guys," she said. "Let's go see Daddy. He's waiting for us."

Dan lifted the hitch of the trailer and began pulling it around the house. The rest followed in single file. They went past the shack and the firepit and hide tanning rack in the back. They reached a clearing that led to a path through the bush. They stepped onto the trail, one by one, to begin this new life nestled deep in the heart of Anishinaabe territory.

They didn't look back.

ACKNOWLEDGEMENTS

I acknowledge and thank the Canada Council for the Arts and the Ontario Arts Council for their grant programs that supported me in the writing of this novel. As an emerging writer, I'm very grateful for these councils and the important work they do promoting and empowering literary voices in Canada. I would never have fulfilled my dream of becoming a published author without these grants.

I am extremely grateful to my employer, the Canadian Broadcasting Corporation, for allowing me to take leave from my duties as a journalist for months at a time to focus on this story and get it written. I am very fortunate to work for an organization that values and supports all my storytelling endeavours.

Thanks also to the Banff Centre for inviting me to their beautiful mountainside compound for two weeks in the fall of 2015, where the writing of this novel began. I'll always remember where I was when I wrote that first sentence on the screen.

The greatest support of all comes from my life partner, Sarah. She's always the first to lay eyes on my written stories, and her critical feedback in those early days is essential. I must give enormous thanks and love to my wife for always being my first proofreader and biggest booster. I would not have made it this far on this path without her support and advice. She motivates me every day to carry myself with honour and respect. G'zaagin!

This story would not have become a novel without the keen eye and editing expertise of the mighty Susan Renouf. She read a first draft years ago while we were discussing another literary project, and decided she wanted to take it on. She believed in this story from the beginning, which filled my heart with promise. Her masterful editing and constructive encouragement greatly bolstered the narrative from start to finish. Huge thanks, Susan.

I must acknowledge and thank the rest of the team at ECW Press, who were nothing but a delight to work with as this book developed and emerged. Everyone has made me feel right at home throughout this process, from editorial to marketing. I couldn't have asked for a better publisher for this project. Gratitude to Jen Knoch and Laura Pastore, who took the last passes at the manuscript and further polished it.

Because the story is set in a fictional location a little farther north than my home territory, I asked the extremely resourceful Derek Fox of Bearskin Lake First Nation to take a look at an early draft. As someone who grew up in northwestern Ontario, he offered very valuable insights that helped me paint a better picture of the community and its unique characteristics and challenges. Chi-miigwech, Derek!

There are bits of very basic Anishinaabemowin scattered throughout this novel. Those words and phrases reflect my own rudimentary understanding of the language, but I did need some assistance with honing in on some specific elements. My brother Mskwaankwad was immensely helpful throughout the writing of this book, answering texts and phone calls and providing his own insights as an Anishinaabemowin teacher. Chi-miigwech n'shiimenh!

The windigo is a looming, often implicit figure in this story. The figure is hinted at, but its image doesn't emerge until closer to the end. The written references are based on stories I heard from elders in my community as I grew up. Many of these stories came from my own father, John Rice, and elder relatives like my aunt, Clara Baker. The dream image of the creature written here is also an homage to legendary Anishinaabe storyteller and author Basil Johnston, who documented important windigo tales in his books like *The Manitous*.

The late Richard Wagamese was a close friend and enormous support who kindly encouraged my writing. There is a long list of Indigenous authors and storytellers who have inspired and mentored me on this journey. They've blazed a trail for aspiring writers like me, and continue to create powerfully important works that are changing the world around us. One I'd like to acknowledge is Richard Van Camp, who offered some vital feedback after reading an advance copy of this book that resulted in the changing of a key detail. He's also a hugely talented and wonderful human being!

Family is everything to me. In recent years we've lost three monumental loved ones who shaped my life around stories. My aunt Elaine Kelly was my first teacher and opened my eyes to the world of Indigenous literature. My grandmother Ruth Shipman was a master orator who made up stories on the spot. My grandmother Aileen Rice shared ancient Anishinaabe tales to build a foundation of culture. They are greatly missed and loved always.

Thanks and big love to my mother, Mona Joudry, my stepparents, grandfather, brothers, stepsiblings, cousins, aunts, uncles, extended family, and friends for their ongoing encouragement.

Finally, I'd like to acknowledge everyone in my life who told me stories and listened to me tell stories. Thanks to Lee Maracle for suggesting this simple yet important gratitude, and for her ongoing guidance and support.